As Shilol
fallen co
he m

I am sorry that I wasn't able to save you. If I had known what had been happening to you since the war, I would have come back sooner. I know I failed you. But I promise you this: Your family will never suffer the same fate. I will keep them safe and see that they live the life that you were denied. Nothing will ever harm Meg or your children.

Even if I have to forfeit my life to protect them, they will *be safe.*

Dear Reader,

I've been asked to tell you about Shiloh and *Shiloh's Promise.* Not an easy thing, since I feel strongly about both the man and his story.

Though I fall a little in love with each of my heroes, Shiloh Butler is special. While I share the emotions of all my characters, I felt his loss, his guilt and his love more intensely. Years later, I still do.

In each book I strive to create characters of principle. Men and women who are not perfect, yet are honorable, even in the face of suffering. For me, Shiloh, a man of integrity haunted by the horrors of his past but still strong, still kind, is the epitome of honor.

A paradoxical mix of steel and sentiment, he is formidable and compassionate. A renegade beyond the trappings of convention. Yet a man of extraordinary gentleness, capable of enduring friendships and even greater love.

Wounded by war and life, Shiloh has scars of body and soul that have left him a man alone. Yet beneath the tough exterior beats the tender heart of one who respects and likes women. Above all, or perhaps because of it, he is a man with promises to keep.

So there you have him. The sort of man who, for me, is the most perfect of imperfect heroes—Shiloh, who strolled onto the pages of *Twice in a Lifetime* one day. Later, building this story around him was exciting. For the first time it was natural to incorporate the elements of danger and suspense I enjoy. He seemed to invite them.

Shiloh, the best of my heroes. *Shiloh's Promise,* the turning point in my writing.

I hope you love him as I do, and enjoy reading his story as much as I enjoyed the writing.

With all good wishes,

BJ James

BJ JAMES

Shiloh's Promise

Published by Silhouette Books
America's Publisher of Contemporary Romance

SILHOUETTE BOOKS

ISBN-13: 978-0-373-36146-5
ISBN-10: 0-373-36146-7

SHILOH'S PROMISE

This edition published by arrangement with Harlequin Books S.A.

Visit Silhouette Books at www.eHarlequin.com

Printed in U.S.A.

BJ JAMES

BJ James's first book for Silhouette Desire was published in February 1987. Her second garnered BJ a second Maggie, the coveted award of Georgia Romance Writers. Through the years there have been other awards and award nominations, including Reviewer's Choice, Career Achievement, Best Desire and Best Series Romance of the Year from *Romantic Times BOOKreviews.* In that time her books have appeared regularly on a number of bestseller lists, among them Waldenbooks and *USA TODAY*.

BJ and her physician husband have three sons and two grandsons. While her address reads Mooreboro, this is only the origin of a mail route passing through the countryside. A small village set in the foothills of western North Carolina is her home.

Prologue

"You're early, Butler." The accusation was thrown by the grim-faced man who stared at Shiloh Butler like a great bird of prey.

"Am I?" Shiloh asked mildly. He glanced at his watch and back at his accuser. One dark eyebrow—the right—lifted eloquently. The left was drawn taut against the scar that slashed like jagged lightning through eye and cheek.

The gentle challenge slipping like a stiletto into the expectant silence brought no change to Sheriff Martin's expression. For a long, calculated moment the sheriff glowered at this hard, dark man who remained unperturbed. Abruptly levering his chair away from his desk, he conceded with grudging respect, "So you're not late; I am." With a subtle challenge of his own he continued, "I have one last call to make, one reference left to check."

"I'll wait." Shiloh's tone was calm, but his eyes were not. And the scar did nothing to dull the intensity of his direct blue gaze.

"Suit yourself." Martin shrugged. As he lifted the telephone, he added in a gruff attempt at hospitality, "Unless you're particularly fond of hanging about doorways, you might as well come in."

Shiloh took a chair by the window. He would wait. He was good at waiting, and watching, and listening. He'd had to be. Once lives had depended on him. Perhaps they would again.

Beyond the windows sounds of the village rose from the street, beating their dusty panes like moth wings. In those sounds Shiloh sensed excitement coursing like an electric current. Trouble had come again to the sleepy town of Lawndale, Georgia. Danger for one of their own. Unthinkable danger for Meg Sullivan and her children.

While area news exploited the plight of innocents in the name of human interest, and citizens gossiped concern in the safety of obscurity, Shiloh came offering sanctuary. Because he was unknown to Meg Sullivan his plan must be accomplished through proper channels. He needed to win the unequivocal approval of one she trusted—Sheriff Barney Martin.

To that end Shiloh knew he must listen and wait, but time grew short. He turned restlessly from the window, concentrating on the voice that droned into the telephone, on each softly accented syllable flowing into the next, on each question laying bare a part of himself.

Nothing was held sacred. Not brutal memories cloistered behind the veil of a rare, black nightmare, nor tragedy that lived with the bittersweet triumph of survival. He listened, as unflinching as granite. The deceptively gentle drawl might have been searching the uneventful past of some faceless nonentity, not adjudging the life and honor of Shiloh Butler.

This was a necessary invasion. Shiloh endured as one accustomed to the consequences of desperate choices, with strength born of patience learned in the steamy depths of a green hell. Yet, after a quarter hour passed and the sheriff still pursued his investigation with unhurried thoroughness, the threads of even that patience began to unravel.

As an exercise in control, Shiloh diverted his attention to his surroundings. Absorbing the shabby elegance of vaulted ceilings and time-worn parquet floor, examining sagging shelves with their astonishing collage of crime and law and tattered classics spilling from them. Then even that trick began to fail him. He found his interest straying to the newspaper that lay on the sheriff's desk, its stark headlines a reproach, the black-bordered photograph of a woman and her children a painful reminder.

He should have come sooner, done more. But he hadn't, and now he might be too late. The bile of an unspoken curse burned in his throat when he realized the telephone rested in its cradle.

Barney Martin leaned toward him, his massive

body supported by hamlike fists. Beneath drooping lids black eyes narrowed. ''All right, son,'' he said in a low rasp. ''I knew you were who you said you were. Anyone who's ever read a financial news rag would. Now, thanks to a couple of senators and a handful of generals, I know you're *what* you say you are.'' He shifted heavily in his chair, the leather protesting violently. Obviously the sequence of checks and cross-checks had ended, and obviously something remained unresolved. With the lessons of hours spent in the company of this agonizingly meticulous man, Shiloh knew the answer would come in the sheriff's own good time.

Sounds seeped again into the room, exaggerated in the hollow stillness. Slanting light sifted through the window. The morning was passing, and each second was precious, but the sheriff wouldn't be hurried. Shiloh realized grimly that both he and trouble had been kept waiting in this dusty little town by a foxy old man, as tattered as his hoard of books, as solid and unpretentious as his office.

Martin abandoned his critical study of Shiloh, turning his attention to the newspaper at his fingertips. With blunt directness he sliced to the heart of his concern. ''What interest do you have in our Meg and her children?''

Shiloh expected his question. He would've been surprised if the sheriff hadn't asked. ''None,'' he answered, ''except to help her. If she'll let me.''

''Yet you say you don't know her.''

''We met once, briefly, at her husband's funeral. She wouldn't remember.''

The sheriff stood, his eyes again probing Shiloh's thoughtfully. Sliding his hands in his pockets, he turned toward the window, his gaze fixed at some distant point beyond the village. ''Before their marriage Keith Sullivan served with you in Vietnam?'' It was a question that needed no answer. Shiloh let the man ramble uninterrupted. ''Spent ten years in the same Vietcong prison. As commanding officer you managed to keep your crew together, lost only one.''

''Yes.'' The admission was dragged from the depths of a hurt that would never heal. ''I lost a man.''

Only a pause indicated that Martin heard the raw ache Shiloh could never hide. After a moment he resumed his inquisition. ''After your release you lost track of Keith.''

''Keith dealt with those years by isolating himself from them.''

Martin nodded as if he understood how painful memories drew some people together and alienated others. ''Three years ago you read the sensationalism that surrounded Keith's murder, came to his funeral, patted Meg's hand, spoke your condolences, then disappeared from her life.''

''That's a pretty fair description of what happened.''

The sheriff rocked back on his heels, slid his hands from his pockets. ''You walk away from her at the hardest time of her life, then reappear nearly three years later with an offer to help.''

''Grief is an intensely personal emotion. A time for friends, not strangers. I was a stranger.''

''What are you now?''

''Danger knows no strangers, only people trying to survive.'' Shiloh's voice took on a hard, grating edge.

The sheriff barely nodded. ''If the situation were reversed?''

''If I had a wife, I think Keith would've come. If not Keith, then someone else.''

''The compassion of the brotherhood of war?''

''I prefer to think it is one human caring for another.''

The sheriff turned to Shiloh. ''This man who's threatened the Sullivans is a certified lunatic, you know.

''In his own twisted way Evan Ballenger considers it justice to take a life for a life. A family for the family Keith killed,'' the sheriff continued. ''After Keith left Ballenger's wife and child to die in a drunken hit-and-run accident, before he could be brought to trial, Ballenger acted like an executioner and exterminated him. Even that wasn't enough. As he was sentenced to an institution for the criminally insane, he vowed to escape, to see done what he called the justice of God. Now he's made good the first part of his threat. He escaped two days ago.''

''Destination Lawndale and the Sullivans,'' Shiloh added grimly. ''He shouldn't find them here.''

''When the news broke I offered to relocate them,

but Meg chose to stay. Dammit, I can't force her. My hands are tied. Legally I can't do anything until Ballenger does."

"I can appreciate her decision. In time of trouble the familiar is security." Shiloh knew, as Meg Sullivan probably did, that this burly old lawman would protect his own as few others could.

"Ballenger's family has influence, pulled some strings, got him into a private sanitorium on the west coast. The way I figure it, with all major means of transportation under surveillance, he's riding his thumb cross-country. If we're lucky that gives us some time."

"If we're not lucky he could be closer than we think."

"Son, you know you'll be dealing with a cunning few sane men could comprehend—"

"I understand," Shiloh interrupted, a hint of remembered dangers in his soft assurance.

Barney Martin nodded curtly. "Then we're wasting time." He reached for his hat. "Let's present your plan to Meg. She'll be expecting us."

Shiloh rose without comment and followed the lawman from the office. No more discussion was necessary. Meg Sullivan and her kids were part of Barney Martin's flock, and he would find the best way to keep her safe. He had decided that way was Shiloh.

A hard-won approval, Shiloh knew, but not final. That decision was, and always had been, Meg's.

One

Meg Sullivan stared out at the departing figure of Sheriff Martin. He had greeted her, said his piece in his fatherly fashion, then hurried away through the bright, shadowless heat. It was midday, and the August sun beat down, burning everything it touched. Meg shivered, wondering if even that fierce heat could warm her.

A sound drew her from her brooding. Faint, muffled, the whisper of cloth against cloth, a drawn breath, a subtle move. She hadn't forgotten the dark and somber man who stood in the gloom waiting. He was hardly a man one forgot.

Sheriff Martin's call hadn't prepared her for Shiloh Butler. Careful assurances hadn't eased the shock of that ruined face, and no description could prepare her for the eyes that seemed to reach into her. There was no other way to describe his magnetism. Halfway across the room, with her thoughts mired in horror, she sensed the presence of guarded strength.

With a hand resting unconsciously over the aching muscles at the nape of her neck, she turned. The frown on her face was less from that ache than from neglect of hospitality learned in childhood. Once, her mother's beloved voice had instructed her. Now, even in time of trouble, hospitality was an integral part of her. "Forgive me, Mr. Butler. I didn't mean to be rude."

"You haven't been, Mrs. Sullivan. You're worried and frightened. I'd like to help if you'll let me."

His voice was like deep, rich silk reaching out to her, striking a spark of hope she dared not nurture. Not yet. The sheriff had been thorough in his briefing. His terse conclusion—*a damn good man*—effusive praise from the taciturn man. But she wanted to know more. A great deal had to be explained before she could place her trust and the lives of her children in the hands of Shiloh Butler. "You say we've met?" Her doubt was apparent.

"Once, long ago."

From the safety of the shadows of the partially shuttered room, Meg let her curious gaze roam over him seeking some memory. From hair as silvery black as her own, down a leanly muscled frame of nearly six feet, he was splendidly male. In the half light his eyes were darker, their penetrating blue enhanced by broken radiance, but the scar that savaged the left side of his face was muted to the faded sepia of an antique photograph. Without its distraction she saw only the unmarked sweep of his forehead and high cheekbones faintly shadowed beneath. His jaw was rugged, his chin barely clefted. When he smiled the flash of his teeth was startling against the bronze of his skin.

Once he'd been a stunningly handsome man. Ironically, the scars that robbed him of that handsomeness branded him with an aura of mystery and brooding sensuality far more fascinating than male beauty. In another place, in another lifetime, she would have found him more than attractive. If they'd met, how could she have forgotten? How did one forget the unforgettable?

Shiloh saw her struggle. He had expected confusion and waited patiently while she searched her mind for some remembrance. When it was clear she could not remember, he explained, ''We spoke briefly at Keith's funeral.''

''You were there?'' The question, bursting from her, was rhetorical. She had no reason to doubt him. ''Were you acquainted?'' A foolish question. Whatever he was, Shiloh was not a ghoul, the sort who had crowded her life then, feeding on tragedy. He would have been a true mourner. Why had Keith never spoken of a friend such as Shiloh? It was an extraordinary omission, yet it explained why she didn't remember. There was little she remembered of the days following Keith's death.

Until the trouble began, her life had been a dream come true. She had a moody but loving husband and two healthy sons. With her first book sold, the second promised and a new baby on the way, there was little more in life she'd wanted. Then Keith's drinking worsened. The dream became a nightmare and her days a futile struggle. She abandoned the last of her stubborn faith in him, certain the worst had come, but in an act of drunken cowardice he'd proved her wrong.

The accident, his flight, had left a woman and her children to die. The murderous rampage of the deranged husband had been too much. Hurt and weary, burdened by guilt, Meg had sunk into the black pall of grief. With her dreams tarnished, she'd gathered her sons around her and wandered in the murky aftermath of death. Even a man like Shiloh had left no mark on her memory. But there was more she didn't understand.

"You're wondering why I came three years ago, and why I've come now." He'd seen the puzzled look as she'd returned to the past and anticipated her question. "Keith and I were together in Vietnam."

"The prison camp?"

"Yes, the camp, too."

In his answer she heard nuances of the horror that had haunted her husband's dreams. "Keith never spoke of that time, nor of the men who were with him."

"Few of us do."

"Yet you've come."

"To help if you'll let me."

"Sheriff Martin seems sure that if anyone can help,

you can.'' She returned to the window, her thoughts on a time of bitterness. ''I wonder if I deserve help.''

''You don't deserve this. No man, however mad, should hold you and the children accountable for Keith's mistake.''

''Poor man,'' she said softly. Her head drooped wearily. ''He's right, you know; I'm as guilty as Keith.''

Her recriminations quivered in the room, falling like stone on Shiloh's ears. He hurt for her, even as he discounted this strange burden of guilt. Meg hadn't harmed Ballenger or his family. He doubted she could harm anyone, but his conviction was of little consequence. Only Meg's mattered, and she held herself responsible in some terrible way.

Someday he would uncover this secret transgression and lay it to rest. Now, he discovered, he wanted only to take her in his arms and soothe her as he would a friend or a hurting child. But Meg Sullivan was not a child; she was a lovely, desirable woman who had lived in his memory for three years.

When Sheriff Martin introduced them Shiloh had been careful to do nothing that would unnerve her, risking no more than a casual study of her. Now as she dealt with what he'd told her he indulged in the luxury of a slow, discovering inspection. She had changed little in three years and was still that incredibly wonderful mix of courage and fragility. He had found her lovely in the past but now, standing before the half shuttered window with the midday sun falling in slanted beams around her, she was more than lovely.

She was a perfect cameo with her features in profile, her hair cascading from a clasp at her nape, curling into an old-fashioned ringlet. From memory he knew her eyes were blue-green, the color of rare turquoise, and the crook at the bridge of her nose was charming. If the jut of her chin was a little strong, the curve of her smile could be gentleness itself. At five feet four she seemed small and delicate to him. Her dress fit without clinging, and its fine-spun fabric skimmed her slender curves. She was a willow before the wind, bending but not breaking. A gallant lady.

Shiloh wanted more than ever to hold her, lifting her bowed head to the light, reinforcing her strength with his. Perhaps in time, if given the chance, he could. ''Meg,'' he said quietly. ''Will you come with me?''

She stepped from the sunlight, moving farther into the room. ''Sheriff Martin says you're a good man with impeccable references.'' She laughed with little humor. ''It sounds as if you're applying for a job.''

''I suppose in a way I am.''

''I wish the sheriff had stayed.'' Indecision trembled in her voice.

''You know why he didn't.''

''He was afraid that if he stayed he might influence me.''

''He's a fair man.''

''But not so subtle as he thinks.'' This time her low laugh was genuine, and Shiloh was encouraged.

''The fact that he left us alone speaks volumes. He trusts you. I wonder if you know how much that means?''

Remembering the intense, almost microscopic scrutiny of his life, Shiloh smiled wryly. ''I think maybe I do.''

Meg's eyes strayed over the strong, immobile features, certain that beneath the composure lay a wisdom that would not discount Barney Martin. ''Yes, I suppose you would.''

Shiloh waited, holding himself in check, as she began to move through the room, touching things, her fingers tracing their shapes absently. At the doorway she paused, the blankness of thought clearing from her face. ''You must be tired of standing, Mr. Butler. Why don't you come into the kitchen for a glass of lemonade while you tell me again about your plan.''

The kitchen was comfortable and revolved around her children. Three growth charts were tacked by the door and a flurry of crayon drawings nearly obliterated the refrigerator. A card bearing names and a profusion of gold stars was mounted by the table—a mother's system of encouragement and reward. Shiloh smiled at the glittering galaxy. Meg had made a wonderful home for her children. She always would, wherever they were.

''Exactly what is this place? What makes Stonebridge and your inn better for us than Lawndale?'' Meg asked, returning the lemonade pitcher to the refrigerator and joining Shiloh at the table.

"It's a small village that's quaint and charming and so far off the beaten path time and most of the world have passed it by. The people are close-knit and old-fashioned and genuinely kind. You'll like them, and they'll like you. There are guests at the inn, but that's another advantage. You'll be guests, too. No explanations needed or expected. For that reason, Meg, if for no other, Stonebridge offers a certain anonymity, and anonymity can be freedom. You can move around freely, within a given area and within reason. As a known quantity Lawndale can't offer that. There'll be no security beyond these four walls. You'll be prisoners for the time it takes to resolve this."

"He can find us in Stonebridge, Mr. Butler."

"No." Shiloh pushed his glass aside, spreading his fingers over the gaily printed tablecloth. "You have no family there and neither did Keith. Only Sheriff Martin will know where you are. When you leave this house you will simply disappear. There's no reason for anyone to connect you with Stonebridge or to me."

"If *he* should? What could stop him then? Here we have the sheriff and his staff. Who would we have there?"

"The staff of the inn, and a governess will see to the children. There will be added security, people trained in protection as few are." He chose not to explain how sophisticated the security network would be, or that he'd brought in people from all over the world. Only he knew that in constructing a cordon of defense he had called in favors he'd never wished repaid, traded on friendships as he'd never done.

Intuition warned that the intensity of what he offered, and the need he felt for it, would frighten Meg more than it could reassure. Meg knew the danger, but for now she needn't know the harrowing complexities the sane mind must confront in anticipating the twisted genius of insanity.

"Meg, I can't work miracles, but I offer the best of my world, and that's Stonebridge. Of all the places in the country, what possible connection would you have with a village tucked away in the foothills of Carolina? If we leave no clues, how could you be found?"

"So we just step into your shiny airplane and fly away to this little Utopia to live happily ever after? You paint a pretty picture, Mr. Butler, but you must forgive me if I have no patience for fairy tales." The anger of helpless frustration that had lain coiled and waiting for days slipped beyond her control.

She rose abruptly, sending her chair tottering against the wall. Her arms were crossed at her breasts, her hands clutching at her shoulders. She'd fought desperately to keep that anger in the background, now just as desperately she was grasping at wisps of shattered control. It was more important than ever before that she make the decisions she must rationally.

"I'm not offering Utopia, nor unending happiness. I wish I could." He answered her sarcasm with soft words, glad for her anger. She'd been unnaturally calm, holding herself too guardedly. This rage could be cleansing, releasing tensions that knotted her body and soothing the pain that must throb in her head. He wished she would scream out her frustration, but beyond this flare of anger there would be no more. Not from this woman. She was too much the fighter, perhaps too much for her own good.

Meg looked down at him, the fury still alive in her eyes cooled by the heat of her outburst. ''Why are you here, Mr. Butler? We're strangers to you. Why would you want to help us?'' In slow, cutting words she demanded, ''What's in it for you?''

''More than you could ever know, Mrs. Sullivan. More than I could ever explain. Just call me a good-deed junkie. Say I get my kicks out of playing the good Samaritan—or, as a dear friend accuses, Sir Galahad.''

His look met hers, holding it. ''Or you might remember, I was there, too. I know what Keith lived with. Some of us came through virtually unscathed. Others came home with time bombs ticking in their heads. Those of us who were more fortunate help if we can, and when it's too late, we help those left behind. I suppose it eases the conscience for surviving when others don't.''

Meg stared at him, suddenly seeing wounds that hadn't healed, something more than lost years and a ravaged face. Shiloh, the survivor, was far from unscathed. She looked away, her anger gone. ''Forgive me, I didn't mean to attack you.''

''Shh.'' Shiloh touched her for the first time. His hand closed over hers, drawing her back to her seat.

"I understand. I meant to help, not add to your troubles."

She liked his touch, the warm strength of his hand closing over hers. She knew in that moment that she trusted this brutally dark enigma of a man. He was the added courage she needed to face the coming ordeal. He would help her keep her children safe, but what of himself? In coming to her he'd stepped into the path of danger. "You could be hurt by this." She touched his scarred cheek with her free hand. "You've been hurt enough."

He turned his face away, moving from her touch. "I won't be hurt, Meg."

Meg was startled by her own presumption. "I'm sorry, I shouldn't have done that."

"Don't be. I've lived with the scar for a long time. I've accepted the curiosity and disgust it causes." He released the hand he held, stroking the scar himself. "Oddly enough, children find it interesting."

Did he think she found it disgusting? Was that why he moved away? Because she could think of no way to make amends she murmured, "The boys will love it."

"Does that mean you'll come with me?"

"We'll come." Her decision brought surprising discoveries. The paralysis of fear was gone, and for the first time in days there was light in her life. She'd struggled with a sickening sense of helplessness, and found herself lost in a cold, empty void with no control, no defenses, and worse, no destination. Shiloh had filled that void with his confidence, presented alternatives, forced her to think. He offered a place to come home to. Its name was Stonebridge.

"A secret hideaway," she murmured, pleased with the description. "I wouldn't agree when Sheriff Martin suggested we should leave Lawndale. Now I see it's the perfect solution."

"Perhaps you should hear what he planned before you make a final decision." Shiloh was aware of how tensely he'd waited for her answer.

"If his plan was better, I'd never have heard yours. You wouldn't have been allowed within miles of us."

"Exactly." He'd never let himself consider what he would have done if she had been kept from him. Thankfully that was one hurdle behind them. There were others. "I'd like to leave as soon as you can manage. Any problem?"

"I assume Sheriff Martin will make whatever explanations my friends will need." She waited for his confirming nod. "Then we have no problem. My work is dependent only on the nearest notepad and the most current deadline. Writing and illustrating children's books can be a very movable occupation."

"Good. Ballenger is coming this way. The airports are being watched, so are the train terminals and bus depots, but he can find other transportation. Our time's running out."

"It seems so strange to hear him called by name," Meg said in a quavering voice. "There are times when I think of him as a monster, not as a poor sick man who lost all he loved."

"Don't fool yourself," Shiloh said sharply. "Evan

Ballenger existed on the fringes of sanity for years, in one kind of trouble or another since he was a kid. He's been a soldier of fortune, a deserter, a junkie and lastly a religious fanatic who beat his wife and abused his children, using his own interpretation of the Bible to excuse his cruelties. The death of his family only precipitated an inevitable madness. He is a monster. You can't let yourself feel sympathy for him; he mustn't have that edge.''

''I know I can't allow the smallest weakness.'' Meg dropped her head into her hands, fingertips at her forehead, thumbs massaging her temples. ''This is so unreal. Sometimes I think it can't be happening to me, that I'll wake up and it will all be a dream.''

He touched her cheek, the smoothness of her skin a reminder of how young and innocent she had remained in the throes of trouble and tragedy. If it was in his power he would see that nothing ever marred that innocence. Evan Ballenger would never touch her with his ugliness. ''This will be over soon. Ballenger's face has been plastered over every major newspaper in the state. He will be recaptured. It may be in a matter of hours; it may be weeks, but it will happen. Until then, we'll keep you safe in Stonebridge, I promise.'' Shiloh stood, his hand still lingering at her cheek. ''Do you believe me?''

''I believe you.'' Meg's heart raced. His confidence was contagious, and he did make her believe. Almost.

He brushed an ebony tendril from her forehead, his fingers smoothing it away, tangling in her hair. The slightest pressure lifted her face to his. Blue eyes, rich, darkening, looked into the tumult of her gaze. Softly he murmured, "Tomorrow?"

"Tomorrow," she agreed, wondering what he sought in her eyes, what he discovered.

Shiloh smiled, and his hold on her hair loosened. He seemed less austere. "Travel light. A small suitcase for each of you, with a favorite outfit or two and any special toys. Anything else can be provided."

"Shouldn't you meet the children?" Meg asked. "Sheriff Martin thought it best they not be here for this meeting but the deputies will have them back soon. Would you like to come by tonight?"

"We can't risk further contact. It's doubtful Ballenger is within a hundred miles of here, but just in case, we mustn't jeopardize our plan. You shouldn't be connected with me. Sheriff Martin strongly suggested I should go to ground myself. He wouldn't approve a second visit." He saw a frown begin on her face and hurried on, "I'll meet the children at the plane."

Meg was surprised when he turned toward the back door, then realized it was part of the precautions being taken for her sake. The deputies had been stopping by in pairs, sometimes off duty and dressed in plain clothes, so it was unlikely her elderly neighbors noticed when the sheriff arrived accompanied by a second man.

Leaving alone, with his battered good looks, Shiloh couldn't hope to escape attention. Thanks to the tall hedge shielding most of her yard, only Miss Hillyard with her opera glasses could report to her fellow gossips that a dark-haired man had left Meg's by the back entrance. Meg hoped the sweet, nosy old lady was taking a nap.

"Until tomorrow, Mrs. Sullivan?" Shiloh stood in the open doorway, the heat of the day creeping past him.

"You called me Meg before."

A half nod acknowledged his slip of the tongue. In his mind she was Meg, never Mrs. Sullivan. "Tomorrow, Meg?"

"Tomorrow," she promised, adding softly, "Shiloh."

Shiloh's plane sat at the end of the quiet airport, blending into the throng of similar aircraft used by commuters who combined metropolitan careers with rural living. The cabin that housed him was comfortable if small. He poured himself a cup of juice from the galley stock before he settled down to work.

He had plans to finalize, calls to make. There could be no better privacy than here. Because time was valuable he coveted the hours lost in formalities. Productive hours, he reminded himself, but lost. If time was valuable, privacy was essential. Though he'd kept a low profile he had been seen on the streets of Lawndale for parts of two days. He wouldn't be seen there again. The schedule for Meg and the children was arranged, and Sheriff Martin would see to its execution. Shiloh's flight plan was filed, the plane readied. After he attended to a few details he had nothing to do but wait. By this time tomorrow, Meg and her children would be in Stonebridge as guests of the inn.

Shiloh sipped the juice, savoring its tartness. From his vantage point he could see any who approached the plane. Satisfied that he was totally alone, he relaxed. From his wallet he removed two folded sheets of newspaper. The first, yellowed and tattered, was a picture of Meg and her sons at Keith's graveside. The second, newer with ink that still stank, was the same. Its story told not of death and tragedy, but of threats to the innocent by an unbalanced mind bent on vengeance.

He had never stopped to question why he kept the first picture. After Keith's funeral he'd folded it, placed it in his wallet and never looked at it again. He hadn't needed to—the image of the Sullivan family had been imprinted indelibly on his mind. The two boys, twins, but not identical, had been a little more than two. Their expressions were bewildered as they held Meg's hands. Meg herself seemed lost and tiny as if shrinking into herself. She had been thin, perhaps the reason the slight swell of her early pregnancy was so prominent.

"I hoped the years would be good to you, Meg," Shiloh said thoughtfully as he held the photographs. "Maybe they have been, until now."

He shifted restlessly, glancing over the field again. Nothing stirred but insects. Sensible, warm-blooded creatures had gone to ground to wait out the rise of the thermometer. He was grateful for the bit of shade that fell from a clump of trees. Since he dared not run any of the systems, the plane was like an inferno. But as the day passed the mercury would be on the downward slide. He'd known worse.

Plucking absently at the soaked shirt plastered to his chest he remembered ten years in a cage in a tropical hell. Irritated, he shrugged the memory aside. It was done, and the consequences were unchangeable. Brooding would serve no purpose. He must concern himself with today's problems, not yesterday's. He carefully refolded the clippings and replaced them in his wallet. From the briefcase at his side he took out a notepad and pen, and ran through the checklists rapidly. Everything and everyone were in place, and all that was needed was his signal.

There were three calls to be made. One to Jeb Lattimer, director of security and surveillance. A second to Alexis Charles, a specially trained governess. The third to Jingo Stark, who would provide transportation for the last leg of their journey.

Three hours and a fourth phone call later he dropped the sweat-dampened receiver on its hook. The first three calls had been business, the fourth pure pleasure. Shiloh stood and stretched, a smile hovering on his face. He'd called to tell Caroline, the best friend he had in the world, that he would be bringing Meg and her children to Stonebridge tomorrow. And, he admitted in total honesty, he'd called to hear of Shiloh Mark, his godchild and namesake.

The papoose, as Caroline and her husband Gabe called him, was just six months old, and from the first moment Shiloh had seen him his heart had belonged to the tiny child. Now that Gabe was out of the country, Shiloh had been charged with care of the Jackson family. These days in Lawndale had been a source of worry. Unnecessary worry, for Caroline was more than competent, she'd spent too many years alone not to be. But that was before Gabe.

"The papoose." Shiloh chuckled, shaking his head as he returned to the galley cooler for more juice. "What a name to be stuck with. It would serve them right if he lifted their hair one day in revenge."

The juice was good. It soothed his parched throat replacing the fluids his body needed. The temperature outside was stabilizing, but the plane seemed hotter than before. A problem easily solved if he could engage the auxiliary systems, but he was determined to draw no attention to himself or the plane. He checked his watch. Only another few hours and the sun would be setting.

He poured a third cup of juice and returned to his seat. He couldn't remember when he'd last eaten, but it didn't matter, he had no appetite. He finished the juice, disposing of the cup in the trash. Pen in hand, he picked up his notes, discovering there nothing more to do. He knew the checklist from memory.

Everything was in perfect order. His people, friends and colleagues, were in place and waiting to begin. Sheriff Martin would carry out his part of the plan to the letter. Everything was better than perfect.

"Why am I so damnably restless?" His voice echoed in the cavernous body of the empty plane. In it he heard the sound of loneliness. "It won't be lonely soon.'' He laughed aloud. ''Not with three rowdy children on board.''

Shiloh's gaze searched the horizon for a sign of twilight. It wasn't for relief he wanted the darkness, but to have done with this day. His restlessness became impatience. He was eager for tomorrow, when he would meet Meg's children.

Two

‘‘Golly! This looks like somebody’s house, not an airplane,’’ a childish voice grumbled. ‘‘Heck! That’s a sofa. Where’s the seats? And the lady who gives you soda like on television.’’

‘‘Telebishum,’’ a baby’s voice parroted.

‘‘Hello, Shiloh.’’ Meg’s greeting was a melody drifting through the spate of sound.

Shiloh turned slowly, delaying the moment that would end a night of agony. His gaze probed the hovering shadows, seeking Meg, finding her.

She stood in the cabin portal, slim-hipped in jeans, a shirt of pale lavender and canvas shoes. Her face was emotionless, the soft line of her bewitching mouth grave. Her hair was a lustrous rope of braided sable. This was the vision he’d waited for the night through. In the graying darkness of predawn she was beautiful.

Two small boys were at her side, one as exuberant as the flame of his red hair, the second a silent, somber, brown-haired version of his twin. In her arms was the loveliest child Shiloh had ever seen—a golden-haired angel of two, who babbled in sleepy-eyed delight over their adventure.

They're all beautiful, Shiloh thought as he tossed aside a final preflight checklist and rose from his desk. He moved toward them through the cabin that did, indeed, resemble a comfortable home. Pausing just beyond their circle he let his gaze drift over each child, lingering long on their bright, curious faces before settling again on Meg.

In the deepening crimson of twilight and the black of a starless night he had reminded himself repeatedly that it was for Keith that he came. For Keith's children—Keith's family. But it was Meg who had haunted him. Meg, afraid and yet brave, who smiled so poignantly it hurt.

"Meg," he murmured, less in greeting than in affirmation that the night of strange, restless dreams had ended.

He'd trained himself long ago to clear his mind of everything, to sleep deeply when he must. Even the nightmare that could hold him in reptilian coils rarely penetrated that iron resolve. A restful, dreamless sleep, once a matter of survival, had become a lingering habit—one that deserted him last night. He couldn't explain this total preoccupation with Meg.

He'd come intending to help. From the beginning he admired and respected her, but the children were his first priority. Then she had touched some dormant part of him, and natural male stirrings had kicked their traces, coalescing into a fierce possessiveness that dared the world to hurt her. Perhaps three years ago he could dismiss his caring as exaggerated sympathy. But today it was a living part of him, as real as the tragedies that brought him into her life. These feelings were an unexpected complication to be resolved, but at another time. His concentration must be complete and all his thoughts for the safety of the children and Meg.

"You're okay?" A question? A wish? He didn't know.

"I'm fine," she answered, her eyes meeting his. "We all are."

"Yes, you are, aren't you?" He was learning that she was almost always composed on the surface with her turmoil hidden far beneath. "Did you sleep the night?" Considering the hour he added ruefully, "What there was of it."

"Enough. Sleep is the least of my needs now."

"You can sleep at the inn. We'll watch over you."

"I know."

"Soon," he said, his gaze still held by hers.

The red-haired imp squirmed, tugging at his mother's hand. The baby girl laughed and babbled. Reminders for Shiloh that they were visible from the field. He cursed himself in silent eloquence. After all his precautions he'd carelessly let them stand exposed while he made clumsy small talk.

"Come away from the blasted door," he lashed out, regretting his harshness the instant the words left his lips. She shouldn't bear the brunt of his anger. The blunder was his. He sighed, then added lamely, "Please."

"Of course. I should have known better." Meg took no offense as she obeyed, stepping farther into the cabin.

Her expression was bland, but Shiloh, keenly attuned to everything about her, saw her breasts rise and fall in breaths so short and shallow they were no more than a tremor. She held herself too straight, her spine too rigid. In the carefully shielded light of the aircraft her eyes were unnaturally bright—only tiny bands of color encircled black pupils. No application of blush and lip gloss, however skillful, could hide her pallor. At the base of her throat a heavy pulse throbbed in the shadowed hollow like the wild heart of a captured bird.

"Can I help?" he asked. "Is there anything—"

"You've done more than enough, Shiloh. What you've offered is our best hope. If there's hope at all." A note of despair crept in. It was a tiny but telling crack in her armor.

Shiloh's first instinct was to fold mother and child in his arms, offering himself as anchor for lives torn asunder. He wanted to tame the savage beat of her heart by putting his lips against her throat. Every part of him ached to protect her. Yet discretion warned that tender words, a kind touch, would bring her house of cards tumbling down. Her cool courage was for her children. For them she faced terror with an apparently unshakable strength. He must do nothing to destroy the costly illusion.

His mind accepted the rules of their desperate game, but his body hungered for the fragile warmth of hers, for the silken touch of her skin. Shaking fingers curled into his palm, and the pencil he'd forgotten broke and fell at his feet. Desire burned like a fever!

This was an impossible situation for him. From this day he could never relax. Every thought and action must be guarded. He'd lived too many years among the ruthless, acquiring the habits of power. He was honest but hard, taking boldly what he wanted. What he took he kept. For as long as he wanted it. He'd never really wanted a woman, not in tenderness, and there had been few women in his life.

Could he live closely with Meg for the days and weeks this might last, wanting but not taking? Could he remain the friend she needed, avoiding unwelcome complications? He honestly didn't know. He'd had no enduring friendships—except with Caroline, and there was never this between them.

Oh God, never this! He took a step nearer, his body tightening, forgetting the children, forgetting danger and promises.

He stopped short. It was as if an invisible wall held him from her. He must not jeopardize their fragile alliance. She was strong in body, far stronger in spirit.

A destructive disparity. He meant to see it would not be. He could be guardian of her physical strength, but mustn't tamper with the inner core that served her so well. He would not add to her troubles or, God forbid, her fear.

Shaking aside feelings deeper than any he had ever known, he forced himself to continue moving toward her, taking one slow step after another when he wanted to run. Deliberately he let his smile touch Meg and each of her children in turn. The attitude he must assume was becoming easier. "Welcome to my home away from home."

"Did you have the door open 'cause you knew we were coming?" the red-haired child asked.

"Certainly. I wanted you to walk straight in and not have to wait on the field." He made it sound like a gesture of welcome, not the precaution it was.

Only the softest scuffle of sound preceded the bulky figure of Sheriff Martin. He loomed behind them, a number of bags tucked under his arms and in his hands. Over Meg's shoulder the men exchanged a look and a nod. All had gone as planned. The unspoken message was balm for frayed nerves, calming the caldron of impatience that had tormented Shiloh for days. The brittle tensions of passive hours dropped away. He was almost jubilant. He could move, he could act. Within the hour the silver aircraft bearing the blue logo of Butler Enterprises would lift toward the gold-rimmed horizon. Their final destination Stonebridge. This was the moment he'd waited for. The moment meant for Meg, her sons and her daughter.

It was a happier man who turned his attention to the children. The grim lines were gone, swept away by his smile. ''From Sheriff Martin's description you must be Edward.'' Purposely addressing the quieter child first and using his proper name rather than a diminutive, Shiloh offered his hand. After a hesitation he pretended not to notice, a small hand was placed in his. He shook it gravely. ''Welcome aboard, young man. My name is Shiloh. I'll be your pilot. I hope you enjoy your flight.''

''Yes, sir.'' Eddie gulped and blushed, then with an uncommon boldness he asked, ''Can I watch you fly the plane, Mr. Shiloh?''

''You certainly may, and you might even be able to help.'' Eddie beamed and Shiloh chuckled, ruffling his hair. ''Thomas,'' he said, shifting his attention to the fidgeting boy, a mock scowl on his battered face. ''You are Thomas, aren't you, not a space pirate come to steal our ship?'' He narrowed his eyes consideringly. ''Space pirates never have red hair. Green, maybe, but never red.''

''Are you a pirate? Is that how you got your eye hurt?''

''Tommy!'' Meg scolded. This was impudent even for her fiery-haired urchin.

''No, Meg,'' Shiloh cautioned. ''Of course he's curious. I imagine Edward is, too. Sorry to disappoint you, fella, but I'm just a plain old man who happens to fly an airplane.'' He touched his scar with the pad of his thumb. ''When I got this I was a soldier in a terrible war.''

"The same as Daddy?" Eddie voiced his curiosity.

"The very same."

"Daddy didn't have a scar." Tommy again, naturally.

"I know." None that showed, Shiloh added mentally. "But the fact remains, I do have a scar. Does that frighten you, Thomas?"

"No, sir."

"Since I don't have green hair, either, shall we shake on it?"

There was no hesitation as the giggling boy slid his hand into Shiloh's, pumping it vigorously. Shiloh smiled in response. "Welcome aboard, Thomas."

"Can I help fly the plane, too?" Tommy asked, no blush beneath his freckles, a cocky grin on his lips.

"Of course you can."

"Can I be first?"

"No. You can help but you can't be first."

"Why not?"

"Because Edward asked before you," Shiloh said, matter-of-factly ending the discussion.

"Oh." Tommy stared wide-eyed at his brother, obviously a little unsettled by this unusual turn of events. Shiloh could see that this twin had been the unconscious leader in their common world. Until today. That Eddie might be first, blazing the trail rather than following, was a new concept that would take much pondering in the days ahead. "Oh, okay." There was a hint of bravado in him. "I need to take care of Mom and Sam anyway."

"Thanks." Shiloh tapped the stubborn little chin

lightly. ''I was hoping you'd say that. You and Edward can take turns watching over your Mom and...'' He paused, one perfect eyebrow lifted. The other, a shattered parody of perfection, did not move. ''This lovely child can't be Sam! Anybody called Sam should have big ears, a red nose and a wart on his chin, not hair like the sun and eyes like stars. This can't be Sam. This is an angel.''

The little girl in Meg's arms chortled, and the boys were howling in laughter. Even Barney Martin had been so entertained he forgot the heavy burden that had long since turned his arms to lead.

Meg didn't laugh. She was closer to tears than laughter, for she'd witnessed something wonderful. In the sunless chill before the dawn, this strange man with the cutthroat's face had warmed her children's hearts. With the wisdom of Solomon he'd approached the boys perfectly. To the shy child he was gently encouraging, to the boisterous one he was carefully firm, and to all he was delightfully amusing. What magic was this? Had he cast his spell over them?

''Come, Meg,'' Shiloh said, ending her distraction. ''Edward and Thomas are going to explore the cabin while Sheriff Martin and I stow your gear away. Take this seat. You must be exhausted.''

''No, not so much.''

''You're so tired you weren't with us,'' he chided gently. ''You were a million miles away.''

''Not quite. I was remembering. It's been days since I heard the children laugh. You were wonderful with them.'' Another facet of this mysterious man.

Her eyes met his, finding a tenderness that unsettled more than it resolved. Tears brimmed, gathering like dewdrops on her lashes. To shield him from the burden of her uncurbed emotion, she hurried on. ''No one has ever understood so quickly before. How could you see so much?''

''I like children. I always have.'' His shrug and the simple reply left more unsaid than it answered, giving rise to a multitude of questions. ''Please.'' He laid a hand on her shoulder. ''Rest.''

Reluctantly admitting her fatigue, Meg let him guide her to a reclining lounge chair. Exhausted by the excitement, Sam had begun to wilt against her. The baby was fast asleep before Shiloh strapped the seat belt around them. Meg heard him murmur something, a faint sound that might be compassion or tender endearment.

Ridiculous! she scoffed, though a part of her admitted it would be wonderful to have someone who cared—really cared. But she mustn't think of it, or attach too much significance to the acts of a genuinely concerned man. There was caring, then there was *caring*.

She sighed wearily. She must think of the children and the ordeal ahead. There was no place in her life for silly fantasies. She would deal with the here and now of reality. Here was the Butler aircraft; now was the beginning of their journey to the promised land of safety. Safety. It was more than a six-letter word, it was a treasure.

With her head on the pillow Shiloh had provided,

she heard the clatter of their cases being stored, the excited exclamations of Tommy, then Eddie, the drawling rejoinders of Sheriff Martin, and Shiloh's replies. After the grueling, watchful silence of the preceding hours the normal sounds of a normal world could almost make her believe her own world was not toppling.

As Sam grew heavier on her breast, and her sweet childish breathing became even, Meg lost herself in the comfort of newfound hope. She meant only to close her burning eyes, but she drifted, instead, into the first dreamless sleep she'd known in days.

"Look at her," Barney said as a hush fell over the cabin. "I wonder how long it's been since she had more than a catnap?"

"Too long," Shiloh surmised. "But I think she'd want to say goodbye."

"Not necessary. You can tell her for me." His beefy hand clasped Shiloh's shoulder. "Take care of them, and watch out for yourself."

"You do the same. Neither of us should forget that a mind like Ballenger's won't deal well with the stress of hide and seek. He could turn on any of us." Shiloh felt a twinge of guilt for the havoc he could be bringing down on the village and the inn. It would be worse for Lawndale. "He'll be coming soon."

"Any minute," Martin agreed tersely.

"Are you ready?"

Martin glanced at Meg and the sleeping child, then at the twins who sprawled in their seats studying the pages of a book of planes. "I'm a lot more ready since you're taking the woman and the tykes to safety. I don't fool myself that I can outguess him. A rational mind, maybe. But Ballenger's smart, cunning and unhinged. It's a triple threat."

"I don't think you'll underestimate him."

"Nor will you."

"I won't be alone."

Martin's black eyes bored into him. "Maybe not, but trust yourself, son. Follow your own instincts. You have a feel for this, and if anyone can get her through this you can. If you weren't such a damnably rich bas—" He broke off, remembering the boys. "Well, anyway, if you weren't, when this is all over I might've offered you a job."

"I might've accepted."

"Phaw!" Martin laughed a belly-shaking laugh, then sobered. "Take care."

"Yeah," Shiloh said softly. "Both of us."

Sheriff Martin had gone. The Butler aircraft was secured. It's engines running, the craft was ready to taxi, then take off. In a change of plans both Eddie and Tommy were seated in the cockpit. Making his final check on Meg, Shiloh knelt by her. His eyes glided over her again and again. He'd never tire of looking at her. If she'd seemed innocent in the broken sunlight of yesterday, in sleep, with her worries tucked away, she was more than innocent. Fragile, delicate, beautiful...this was Meg.

Her braid had loosened. A gleaming tendril was teased by the breath of the sleeping child. Silken lashes lay like a web against her cheeks. Her skin was translucent, too pale beneath the blush, but so soft, so fine. Shiloh felt the familiar ache, the need to hold her. And more, he admitted. He was neither a saint nor a monk. He wanted Meg Sullivan.

Her head moved restlessly, and a frown line appeared between her brows. She moaned softly. Without thinking Shiloh slid his hand beneath her braid, his fingers finding the taut cords of her neck. With the tips of his fingers he massaged the tightness away. Long after the frown disappeared he stroked her skin. Her whimper of pleasure sucked the breath from him, making his own pulse pound like the wings of a captured hawk.

He jerked his hand away, fearful that he woke her, relieved when he saw he hadn't. It was the child who roused. She shifted, nuzzling into her mother's breast, and a thumb popped into her mouth. As her eyes closed again, so did a chubby fist around the braid that had fallen over Meg's shoulder. Shiloh crouched there debating. In the end, deciding Meg must rest undisturbed, as carefully as he could he extracted the woven black satin from the baby fingers.

"Shiloh?"

"Uh-huh," he murmured, intent on his task. "I didn't mean to wake you."

"Did you?" Meg asked, sleep slurring her voice.

"Almost." He chuckled. "But if we're both careful I think you can sleep again."

"The boys?"

"With me."

''Oh.'' She breathed deeply, her breasts rising, pushing against her blouse. ''Then everything's fine.''

''I hope so,'' Shiloh muttered, then realized that she was already asleep. He rose to tower above her, his hand touching her cheek. She was more than delicate, more than beautiful. She was incredibly and almost unbearably desirable. With a look from her, or a touch, or even the simplest gesture, the fever of unreasoning passion erupted in him like a violent compulsion.

He came to protect her from Ballenger. Who would protect her from him?

The helicopter chopped through the air, gliding in a swift path over power lines that crisscrossed the rolling terrain. No blue logo decorated the scarred sides of this craft. It bore instead the mark of an electric power plant.

''Having fun, kids?'' The young pilot flashed an engaging smile at the boys who shared the seat beside him.

''Yeah,'' Tommy answered. ''Do you do this every day?''

''Most every day,'' Jingo Stark shouted above the din of rotors and the rush of their pressure.

''Must be fun,'' Eddie volunteered a rare comment.

''Not when it snows. Then it's colder than a wizard's whistle up here.'' Jingo laughed. ''Thank goodness we don't get much snow.''

''When we do, it's a lulu and, freezing or not, you work like a dirty dog searching for downed lines, making sure no one goes without electricity,'' Shiloh commented from a back seat. ''Don't let him fool you, kids. Jingo's saved more than one life with his chopper.''

''Aw, Shiloh,'' the young man protested, his face flushed beneath the bill of his baseball cap. Praise from Shiloh Butler, the hottest ace in 'Nam until his capture, was praise indeed. ''I just do my job.''

''And more,'' Shiloh added, leaning forward, his hand gripping Jingo's broad, bony shoulder. ''You've lost weight. You need to come by the inn and let the chef fatten you up.''

''I'll do that. Look, ma'am.'' Jingo banked the craft and dipped below tree level. His smile was neither as rakish nor as boyish as those meant for the twins or Shiloh. Instead there was hint of concern for the pretty, sad-eyed lady who'd sat quietly throughout their journey. ''This little body of water is Crystal Lake. If my blades don't rough up the water too much you can see why.

''The larger, darker lake over there is Quarry Pond. Nobody knows why the littlest is called a lake and the largest a pond.''

Reluctantly Meg drew her gaze from the mesmerizing pattern of clouds on the horizon, and her mind from the numbing netherworld of thoughtless daydreams. Obediently she leaned forward, her chin brushing Samantha's curls. She made no comment, having long ago given up on conversation. Tommy and Eddie were much too fascinated with the dashing Jingo Stark and, even if the noise inside the small cockpit hadn't been prohibitive, Shiloh seemed ill-disposed to small talk.

He'd been withdrawn and distant since they'd deplaned in Atlanta. She'd entertained and as quickly dismissed the speculation that he was uneasy when not at the controls. His respect for Jingo was too real for that. She'd wondered briefly if he regretted the deep commitment he'd made to their safety, and knew she was wrong again. There was pleasure in his manner when he dealt with the boys and with Sam. It was only when he looked at her that there was frost in his eyes.

"Do you like it?"

"I beg your pardon?" Her voice was raspy from disuse.

"Crystal Lake?" Jingo dipped the helicopter so low spray from a waterfall misted around them. "Do you like it?"

"Of course," she replied hastily, just realizing that the young pilot had made this detour for her. A gift, to draw her from her isolation. The perfect gift.

Through the window she could see a small lake fed by a low waterfall. Beyond, joined with it by a rocky stream, was a larger lake, its waters dark azure. Willows and stunted dogwood lined the rocky banks. "It's beautiful! So clear! Is that bedrock I see?"

"Sure is." Jingo grinned. "This used to be an old quarry. Crystal is shallow with ledges near the shore. The quarry pond has walls that are solid rock and straight down. It's murky and deep, and cold." He stressed the word for the benefit of the boys. "Crystal has the clearest water in the state, though. Toss a nickel in it, you can see it a month later.''

''Can you swim in it?'' Tommy asked.

''In Crystal Lake you can. But the pond is too steep and too deep. That's cramp city for sure.''

''Have you? Been in the pond, I mean?'' Eddie turned his gaze from the pale green water below to the darker water beyond, and finally to the face of his newest hero.

''Once, on a dare. Let me tell you, I promised the good Lord if he'd let me out of there I'd never do it again. I tell you true, by the time I crawled and clawed up that slippery cliff I was as blue as a Carolina sky. Don't ever try it.''

''Yes, sir,'' the boys answered in unison.

''Let me tell you why. Once I knew a fellow who...'' Jingo settled into his tale, enthralling his audience.

As the helicopter banked again and rose Shiloh leaned back, letting his gaze drift over the countryside he loved. The low-lying hills were a patchwork of field and forest. The red of freshly tilled soil was a perfect foil for the deep green of pine and oak. This was the third leg of their journey, and the last. They were almost home. He smiled and drew a deep satisfied breath, his gaze inadvertently meeting Meg's.

''Comfortable?'' He mouthed the word. As her gaze touched his lips, reading them, there was the dreaded rush of sensations. He'd been lulled into a false sense of the security by Jingo's chatter and by fatigue.

He was powerless before the hungering he'd thought to exorcise by sheer willpower. His defenses crumbled like brittle clay, and he was caught in the snare of forbidden desire. As her eyes lingered on his lips he struggled to resurrect a wall of resistance. When he could speak again there was a rime of ice in his eyes and in his half shout as he asked again, "Are you comfortable?"

"Yes, thank you," she answered almost primly. For the tiniest instant he'd been as he was at the first of their journey. Then in a heartbeat he changed. "What—" she began and found she hadn't the courage to ask what she'd done.

"What?" Shiloh prompted, watching her face, discovering exactly how imperfect his resistance was.

"Nothing," Meg replied. "It's just that you seem troubled."

"Except for Ballenger I haven't a care in the world." He managed a smile that was as much a lie.

He was anything but fine. He was hot and hurting and out of control. Angrier with himself than he'd ever been. Angry that her forlorn face with the bruises of weariness beneath her eyes could melt the cold seclusion that contained him. Angry that with one trembling smile his last refuge was destroyed. Angry that his blood pounded, that a multitude of sensations knotted his gut and clouded his mind. He was angry at the anger that disturbed and hurt her.

He bore little resemblance to the Shiloh Butler reputed to be cool and calm under any fire. To Meg he must he a confusing stranger, snapping and snarling at the least provocation. She had every reason to doubt the wisdom of trusting her life and the lives of her children to him.

Suddenly he curled her hand in his. "Talk to me," he commanded. Even shouting above the helicopter's engines was better than guilty silence. His grasp tightened.

"What would you like me to say?" She was clearly astonished by the abrupt change.

"Whatever your heart desires," he growled. "Just talk."

She was quiet for a long time, searching his face for the nature of his strange malady. Shiloh was anything but mercurial, at least not usually. She believed that as much as she believed in his strength. "All right." She cast around frantically, seizing on the first subject that came to mind. "Do you always arrive by helicopter?"

Shiloh sighed and relaxed. This would work. "I usually fly the jet. There's an airport an hour's drive from the inn. Our flight from Lawndale to Atlanta, the charter to the power plant and our flight with Jingo have been strictly precaution."

"You flew directly into Lawndale, didn't you?"

"From Atlanta. Point of origin would tell Ballenger nothing; destination would." Unconsciously his thumb stroked the back of her hand. "I won't make a mistake that would endanger you, I promise to keep you safe."

Even from myself. For a stunned moment he thought he'd said the words aloud.

Her gaze was unwavering and for once unwary. "You couldn't hurt me, Shiloh."

Somewhere in the conversation they had forgotten to shout. As their voices softened Meg leaned closer. Her fragrance surrounded him in a beguiling bouquet of jasmine and wild roses, and the cap slipped from the volcano within him. Thickly, hardly aware he spoke, he muttered, "Meg, sweet…"

"Castle!" Samantha, who had slept and babbled and slept again, chose this time to assert herself. Bouncing lightly on her mother's lap she cried again, "Castle."

"The inn," Shiloh corrected. An incredible sense of homecoming swept through him, and the fires of the volcano were banked and left to smolder. Sudden laughter filled his face. "Home, Samantha."

"You love this place, don't you?" Meg was fascinated by the shifting kaleidoscope of his moods. There had been gentleness and courage. He'd been brooding and tender, even angry and forbidding. Until now there hadn't been real laughter.

When he laughed he was breathtaking.

"Mr. Shiloh." Tommy struggled against his seat belt to peer out the window. "Who are those people down there?"

"They're my friends," Shiloh said. "They'll be yours, too."

Jingo busied himself with the controls. The helicopter began to descend. Before the dust began to rise beneath the beat of the propeller blades Meg caught a glimpse of a tiny red-haired woman and a willowy blonde.

Two stunning women waited for Shiloh. Her gaze dropped to the dark strong fingers entwined with hers. Why then, after his brooding indifference, was it *her* hand he held?

Dust was a red fog around them, the noise nearly intolerable. Jingo's monstrous machine touched ground as lightly as a floating thistle.

Three

Distracted by the direction of her thoughts, Meg was startled by a rush of activity in the cockpit. Seat belts were unclasped, doors flung open, and before Meg could forbid it, the twins scrambled eagerly out of the craft.

Jingo plucked the baby from Meg's arms just seconds before Shiloh lifted her from her seat. As her feet touched ground, his hand hovered for awhile at her midriff, barely beneath her breasts, steadying her. The intimate touch was stunning, electric, and an undefined nuance became an awakening. With her body singing for his, Meg was feverishly aware of Shiloh. His vitality; the texture of his skin against her own; the steely strength in sinew and muscle of arms that had held her; the gentle gallantry; the secret brooding; his dark, passionate maleness.

The fire, the ice, the gentle and the bitter, these were the enigma of Shiloh.

The heady scent of him, the essence of sunlight and mystery, seemed to reach through the dusty heat surrounding her, holding her. She swayed toward him, the fullness of her breasts brushing his chest.

"Careful." The word was ground out through lips set in a grim line. His fingers convulsively closed again around her.

"Sorry. The world doesn't seem quite steady." She made the breathless excuse with her eyes downcast, hiding the lie.

"It'll take time to get your land legs back," he said in a smoother voice. "Just take it easy."

She expected those hard, rough hands to slide from her keening body. Instead they lingered, searing her with their possession. His head bent slowly to hers, his gaze touching, caressing. There was no gentleness in the dark blue stare, and within them something primal moved beyond its genesis.

"Shiloh?" There was the trembling of her clamoring heart, her bewilderment, in his whispered name.

Nothing about him moved. Only the pulse at his temple throbbed, each beat faster than the last, outracing its own wild tempo. She thought to tame it with her fingertips. He flinched at the contact but didn't move away. Like the swoop of a marauding hawk his hand captured hers, holding it against his cheek. His breathing was low and labored, his eyes fierce. His grip was crushing, driving the gold band she wore into her flesh.

The cutting pain belonged to another hand. It was irrelevant, a small ripple in the still, sensual water she trod. Every sense was commanded by Shiloh. He was rare wine, and she was the crucible. What was pain when he was a part of her?

A bolt of longing blazed through her like summer lightning. Nothing in her life had prepared her for its seething intensity. A sigh shivered in her, her lips parted, her captive fingers moved in a caress against his skin.

No!

The guttural cry that shattered her heart was never made. It found voice in the grimness of his face, in the way his head was flung back, his black hair flying like the mane of a wild stallion eager to run. His hand loosened, slipping from her as he stepped away. Fingers curled into fists, and Meg saw anger in him. His chest heaved, the rasping breath held hostage in his struggle for control, then he was as still, as unyielding as marble. In the little time it took his scornful rejection to tarnish her wonder he was transformed.

The change was sudden and overt. The rigid cords of his neck relaxed, the stiff, unnatural angle of his shoulders eased, the breath sighed softly from him. Anger vanished. When their gazes met again there was no fire; neither was there ice. Shiloh wore an indifferent mask.

Belatedly pain asserted itself, arching through her crushed fingers in welcome confirmation of her existence. The chill of an arctic wind swept through her, cooling flames to embers and embers to dusty ash. But for the throb of her hand the interlude might never have happened. Had it—except in her mind? The sensual storm had been so intense it hadn't occurred to her that he might be immune to its sweeping force.

How could you not feel it? she wanted to cry out. *Dear God! Shiloh, how could you not?*

She risked a look, seeking some hint of that incandescence or even the wintry cold, but if Shiloh was disturbed he hid it behind a visage of tranquility. The moment hadn't been shared. It had been caprice, and hers alone.

He had reacted violently, moving from her touch with a sort of desperation. Once before, in the quiet of her kitchen, he moved away less dramatically when she stroked his scar in sympathy. Much as she might wish to think it, his scar was not the problem. He had lived so long with it that it had become a natural part of him.

No, it wasn't the scar. It was her touch, the sympathy it implied, that he found objectionable. For Shiloh sympathy was intolerable. Only the rarely privileged friend or the beloved could offer it. She was neither.

Remembering where they were Meg reached into herself, mending the tatters of her elusive dignity. As she turned from him to the people who waited she braced herself, expecting their distaste for the scene she'd played. Her bravado was wasted, there was no pitying audience.

The women, a huge man and a boy in uniform were moving onto the landing pad. Prudently they'd kept a respectful distance from the churning dust and had witnessed none of her humiliation. Shocked, Meg realized the incident had taken place in the space of a heartbeat. No one was aware of what passed between them.

As if waiting for her cue—for the flying debris and Meg to be settled firmly on the ground—the flame-haired woman rushed to Shiloh. Her smile was radiant, and a kiss landed haphazardly on his chin. Chuckling ruefully at the result of her unbridled enthusiasm she declared, ''Welcome home.''

Shiloh's arms closed around her, nearly hiding her from view. His lips touched her forehead. ''Hi, tiger.''

The whole group burst upon them. The blonde, Meg learned, was Alexis Charles, a gorgeous and most unlikely governess. The tall man with his wonderful face framed by long, golden hair and a Van Dyke beard was Jeb Lattimer, head of security, second in command only to Shiloh. The bellboy was Tim. Last was the spirited Caroline Jackson, who remained beneath the shelter of Shiloh's arm.

Flashing Meg a perfect smile, Alexis drifted away to take Sam from Jingo. Jeb gave a short, concise report to Shiloh then walked to the helicopter to unload their luggage. Under Alexis's watchful eyes the twins tumbled over the meadow burning off the energy of excitement. Meg felt distinctly superfluous as Caroline and Shiloh exchanged homecoming gossip.

"How is Shiloh Mark?" Shiloh asked.

"The papoose is terrific." Caroline slanted a mischievous glance at him. "Bessie Streeter's watching him."

"Someday he'll live up to the name and leave a wide part in your hair." Shiloh laughed. "With two perfectly good names you saddle him with something as awful as papoose."

"It is terrible, isn't it? But I'm a creature of habit."

"Predictable is the better word, and you're doing it again, Caroline. Chattering to hide something." His tone softened. "Have you heard from Gabe?"

"Yesterday. The dam can be salvaged." Her voice trembled. "The terrorists didn't do as much damage as first thought."

"You're scared stiff for him." Shiloh drew her closer. "The loneliness is hell." His head rested on her flamboyant curls. "He'll be all right."

Caroline moved out of his embrace smiling that same radiant but fragile smile. "I know, and I know he had to go. Africa isn't the other side of the moon, and in less than six weeks he'll be home with Pete and Mark and me." She chuckled, an unexpected, delightful sound. "Did you hear? I called the papoose Mark. He won't have to scalp us after all."

Meg watched, fascinated. Shiloh guided Caroline through despair so naturally, Meg wondered if either realized. There was in Shiloh a tenderness as rare as it was wonderful, and she found herself seeing him through different eyes.

Sheriff Martin had called him fair and honorable, a good man, and if necessary, a dangerous man. He'd met the challenges of Vietnam with a cool detachment that preserved his humanity, and a proficiency that won respect. As a prisoner he'd plotted and schemed for the survival of his men, clawing his way through starvation and torture. Clinging to shreds of that humanity he emerged a hard man, wounded emotionally and physically, but with his sanity and his honor intact.

Nothing about him surprised Meg. Except the gentleness that should have been destroyed long ago. Once, in what seemed another lifetime, she'd wondered how a man so ruthless could be so tender. Now she wondered how a man of such great tenderness could be ruthless.

"Tell me about this." Shiloh traced a line down a grease-smudged cheek. "Troubles closer to home?"

"Nothing I can't handle." She laughed, then rocking onto her tiptoes she kissed his cheek. "I'm glad you're home, old friend. I needed one of your famous pep talks." Stepping out of his embrace she turned to Meg. Her smile was no longer fragile. It was warm and uninhibited. Taking Meg's hands in hers she exclaimed, "Welcome to our village, Meg Sullivan. I hope you find peace with us."

Meg inclined her head, looking into dancing eyes that were more silver than gray. "I think I will. Shiloh painted an enticing picture."

A hearty laugh seemed to rise from Caroline's toes as she shoved her hands in the back pockets of her jeans. ''He's incurably prejudiced, but it's a nice village. Our innkeeper extraordinaire adds to its charm.''

''Our jack-of-all-trades is our greatest distinction.'' Shiloh scrubbed at the grease on Caroline's face. ''You can see she dresses the part.''

Caroline's red hair swung around her shoulders in a cloud of fire, and a finger tapped her temple. ''I knew I was forgetting something. If you're with us long enough you'll find formality isn't my strong suit. I intended to apologize.'' She looked at her rumpled clothing. ''Not exactly haute couture for meeting someone for the first time, but I have a bulldozer down, been wrestling with it all morning. If Jingo has the part I called for, then I'm back in business.

''Meg, I'll call you. We'll have lunch, and I promise to look better. Shiloh, I'm glad you brought her to us. And for heaven sakes, don't keep her standing in the hot sun.''

Like a whirlwind she was around and away leaving Meg astonished. ''Did she say bulldozer?''

''She did. She drives them, repairs them, she builds houses, fights fires, and is the most talented self-trained architect I've ever known.''

Meg was ready to believe anything. ''Caroline is a fireman?''

''Uh-huh, that's how she met Gabe. Fell off the roof of the inn straight into his arms.''

Meg shuddered, remembering the steep gables of

the roof Samantha thought resembled the castles in her book of fairy tales.

"It's a long story. Someday I'll tell you about Caroline. The years she spent waiting for Mark Donovan. Not sure if she was wife or widow, raising their son, Pete, alone. How grief over Mark's death nearly destroyed her until Gabe Jackson caught her in his arms and refused to let her go."

"Then he gave her a son named for both you and Mark," Meg ventured.

Shiloh chuckled, his eyes sparkling. "You'll meet the papoose soon. Now we'd better do as Caroline said and get you out of the sun."

Meg followed his lead, wondering what other surprises were in store for her. Could there be more than a red-haired tomboy who made her feel special; or a governess suited for the cover of *Vogue* or an amber-eyed, bearded Adonis who could do as much for the cover of any magazine? Could there be more than Shiloh, the greatest surprise of all?

Her mind was awhirl as she waved goodbye to Jingo and joined the Pied Piper procession to a waiting van.

The sun lifted over the horizon. Meg had waited for it, watching as darkness became light. Yesterday the inn had been a morass of names and faces and picture-postcard charm. Too much happened too quickly, until her reeling mind had drawn a veil around itself, blurring the richness, tempering the excitement. She'd moved like an automaton through the ritual of settling the children into their suite, too exhausted to be hurt or even grateful that they hadn't needed her comfort. Finally, commanded by Shiloh, she stumbled to her bed and at a ridiculously early hour fell into dreamless sleep.

Revived by a superabundance of rest, she woke without the nausea of dread churning her stomach. Feeling almost weightless without the oily tension she'd become so used to she stood at her open window breathing the unsullied perfume of the dew-drenched world. As its tranquillity enfolded her she knew the inn was everything Shiloh promised.

Built of slate and stone, it nestled in a cozy glen that bordered a tumbling stream. Clusters of river birch dotted the carefully tended lawn, flowers and ivy lined the meandering walks, a rustic fence guarded horses that grazed a velvet meadow. Circling like a fortress was a forest of whispering pines, their deep green crowned by the misty blue mountains that towered in the distance.

Meg felt the first, frail stirrings of contentment. In an adjoining room her children slept under the watchful care of Alexis Charles. With the added sense of security the efficient and affectionate young woman afforded, Meg could spend this hour finding serenity in a spectacular southern dawn. She could put aside her troubled thoughts of Keith and needn't cope with guilt. For a precious time she could forget her husband, the stranger who drank and stopped, then drank again and did not stop. She could remember Keith, her lover, the father of her children.

''I failed him. We failed each other. But there were good times, too.'' The words were simple yet Meg felt as if she had taken a small step forward out of the darkness. Her smile was suddenly radiant. Not even the threat of Ballenger could spoil the discovery that happiness could abide with guilt. She laughed, her arms lifted as she embraced her first real day in Stonebridge.

The door behind her swung stealthily open, a board creaked, a giggle was smothered by the clap of a hand and suddenly her children were around her. ''S'prise.'' Samantha wound her arms around Meg's knees. ''S'prise, Ma, s'prise.''

With Eddie a half step behind him, Tommy did a war dance around the room, screaming into the bedlam, ''We've been awake forever but Lexis made us wait. She said you were zausted. Now we're going down to breakfast and Lexis promised we could slide down the stair rail.''

''Wanta slide, too,'' Samantha demanded.

Meg bent to scoop her into her arms. With the child settled comfortably on her hip she kissed each boy in turn. ''Breakfast sounds terrific, but I don't know about the rail.''

''Lexis said Shiloh wouldn't mind.'' Eddie made his contribution to the conversation.

''Lo Lo not mind,'' Samantha declared emphatically.

''He won't, huh?'' Meg stepped away from the window. ''Well, Alexis, can you watch these wild Indians for a little longer? Until I get dressed?''

"Of course," Alexis assured her from the doorway. "We'll wait for you at the stairs. The bottom."

"I won't be a minute." She kissed the children again and shooed them on their way. As she closed the window she didn't notice the man on horseback who watched from the shade of a tall pine.

Shiloh hadn't meant to spy. He'd simply paused in his daily routine and found himself captivated.

When he was at the inn, his day began with Dakota. In the cool, young hours of the morning the great black horse loved to race over the meadow. Like a colt he splashed through the rocky stream, trampling over small shrubs that hovered against the ground like murky puddles. At the crest of the hill that overlooked the inn, the half-wild stallion took control and Shiloh braced for the run through the forest.

Shiloh relished the challenge. As the horse threaded through the narrow maze of straight-trunked evergreens, a whirling missile with pounding hooves muffled by a half century of carpeting pine straw, only the creaking of the saddle betrayed that Shiloh rode like a Cossack to keep his seat. At the edge of the clearing he drew the horse to a halt, elated.

"It's always the same, isn't it, boy?" Shiloh leaned to stroke the bowed neck, his body loose in the saddle. "No matter how fast or how hard you run, you're always ready for more." He understood the exultation, the eagerness for more. Speed and danger and the hard work simply to survive burned away energy and caged frustrations. They were both caged. Dakota by the miles of fencing that surrounded the meadow. Shiloh by the past, his fence the rules of convention.

"Here in the forest you don't have to be tame, do you?" And I prove that I'm not quite so civilized after all, he thought. Dakota snorted as if to emphasize that neither was docile. In a high-stepping dance he strained at the bit. "No more today, fellow. I have guests who need my attention."

His eyes involuntarily sought the window he knew was Meg's. It was then he saw her. His easy posture deserted him until he realized that in the long shadow of the pine he was virtually invisible. It was the dawn that had drawn her to her window. The countryside that enthralled her.

"God help me, Dakota, she's beautiful." His voice rasped from a throat gone dry. Dakota snorted again and tossed his head, then sensing a change in Shiloh he was still.

Meg's simple yellow gown was like a splash of sunlight, baring her arms beneath lacy sleeves. Her face bore the tawny blush of sleep, and her black hair gleamed with unsuspected highlights of silver and gold. Beneath the gauzy fabric her breasts rose as she inhaled the fragrance of the morning. Her gaze lifted to the blue-misted mountains.

She looks right, as if she belongs, Shiloh thought. Watching her he saw her lift her face to the sun, and he saw her smile. Impulsively he raised his hand to wave when suddenly she turned, bent from sight, then rose holding Samantha. The baby's chubby arms were around Meg's neck, burrowing beneath the tangled gossamer of her hair. There were shouts of laughter, and he knew that Thomas and Edward were with her. As abruptly as it began the laughter stopped.

The sound that drifted through the window had been a faint ripple over the deserted lawn. Shiloh found it enchanting. When it ended the silence suffocated. His isolation was total when Meg closed the window and turned away. The gold of the sun turned to dross, and his exuberance became the defiance of a lonely man. He and Dakota shared complete harmony because they were misfits.

Dakota should run free like the wild stallion he was, ranging the grassy plains of the Badlands of his namesake. Gathering his harem of mares, breeding powerful sons and daughters. Instead he'd been passed from owner to owner, fighting longer and harder against each, until he'd been labeled unmanageable and scheduled for destruction.

In a chance encounter Shiloh saw in him a kindred spirit and brought him to Stonebridge. Now he grazed lush southern pastures and allowed something as insubstantial as a split-rail fence to contain him.

"Captivity, castration of the spirit." Shiloh didn't know if he spoke aloud or if the words were a brand on his brain. He knew, though, that he spoke of himself more than the horse. The years in a jungle prison had destroyed some integral part of him. The scar on his face was only the visible wound.

Something was missing. It set him apart, preventing a natural life. He had friends, cared passionately for them and their well-being, yet solitude was his destiny. He would never know the special sharing that made a man whole.

His heart was as sterile as his body. He was incapable of falling in love.

In the years of freedom his sexual liaisons had been brief and uncomplicated. He'd wanted little—the pleasure of an attractive woman on his arm, the company of a congenial dinner companion, a willing anodyne for a basic physical need—a woman he liked and respected. There was never more. His heart remained untouched.

"Then there was Meg."

Dakota turned at the sound of his voice, swinging his head to nip at the toe of a boot. He made a low rumbling sound, questioning Shiloh's strange mood.

"I know." Shiloh abandoned his melancholy reverie, not quite ready to explore the madness of it. "Instead of wallowing in sentimental drivel, I have guests who need me, and you have a nice, tame filly to court." He nudged the horse lightly, letting him canter to the corral.

Shiloh paused in the doorway of the dining room. With a shake of his head and a small wave of his hand he tried to dismiss the hostess who was inclined to hover. She was patently inefficient, even for a summer temporary, but to her credit she tried, and Shiloh hadn't the heart to fire her. Extricating himself as diplomatically as he could he sent her to greet the newest arrivals. Then the bumbling young woman was forgotten as his searching gaze found Meg.

She and Alexis were entertaining the children over breakfast. As he watched them, feeling rather than hearing Meg's laughter, his body began to throb in a ragged, sensual rhythm. "Dammit!" he muttered and ignored the startled look of a departing guest. "Why?"

Why did Meg, who made none of the ritual man-woman gestures, have this effect on him? Even when she looked at him, her eyes filled with the kind of pity he abhorred, his response was the same. It was insane that with a look, a smile, and God forbid, a touch, she turned him into a quick-tempered tomcat with unsheathed claws.

"I will not hurt her." The familiar litany poured like a broken record through clenched teeth. "By all that's holy, I promise I will not hurt her."

"Morning, boss," Alexis called as she spotted him. "Daydreaming?"

"Something like that," he answered, altering his grimace to a smile and weaving his way through the crowded room to their table.

"Shiloh!" the twins yelled enthusiastically.

"Good morning, boys." He touched each on the shoulder. "Good morning, sunshine." With a finger he stroked the dimpling cheek of the baby and turned to Alexis. "Any problems?"

"Not one. These are perfect kids."

"Hardly," Meg protested. "They're normal, not perfect."

"That's even better," Shiloh said, letting his gaze fall on her at last. "Did you rest well?"

''We all did.''

''You were awake early.''

Meg was startled. ''How on earth did you know?''

''I saw you at your window.''

''I watched the sunrise. You were right, Shiloh. This is wonderful.''

''Were you and Dakota out this morning?'' Alexis asked. At Shiloh's nod she predicted dourly, ''One day you two are going to kill yourselves.''

Meg looked from Alexis to Shiloh in alarm. ''What do you mean?''

''Dakota's a black demon of a horse, bigger than any quarter horse has a right to be.''

''You exaggerate, Alexis.'' Shiloh laughed as he hooked an extra chair from a nearby table and sat uninvited.

''Only a little,'' Alexis said, then laughed. ''Well, maybe a lot.''

''Is Dakota an Indian horse?'' Tommy asked.

''His ancestors maybe, but not Dakota.''

''Maybe he is,'' Alexis said. ''It could be the reason he hates a saddle.''

The idea of a horse hating a saddle intrigued Tommy, and he clamored for an explanation so vigorously that Meg placed a restraining hand on his arm. ''Tommy, you're forgetting there are other guests.''

''It's just as well he asked,'' Shiloh said. ''The barn and the corral are off limits without strict supervision, but they should still understand about Dakota.

''Edward.'' He addressed the quiet twin first.

"Thomas. You don't need to be afraid of Dakota. There's not a gentler animal around, but he hates to be penned up and he gets a little panicky about a saddle."

"Except when you're in it," Alexis amended.

"That's true. And I don't ever intend to leave him saddled and unattended, so we don't have any worries, do we?"

"No, sir." Tommy and Eddie answered in unison.

"Good! Then that's settled." Turning to Alexis he asked, "Have you spoken with Jeb this morning?"

"When we first came down."

"We slid down the banister," Tommy interrupted with a proud warble.

"Down, down," Samantha crowed.

"Sounds like fun." Shiloh slanted a mischievous glance at Meg. "Did your mom slide, too?"

"Of course I didn't!"

"But you'd like to," he teased.

Meg blushed. "It looks like something out of Tara. All that's missing is Scarlet, but it is tempting. Maybe once, before I leave."

"Then you shall." Shiloh was pleased by the lilt in her voice. Once she'd been afraid to look to the future.

"If you two will excuse us." Alexis pushed back her chair and stood. "The children and I are going to explore."

"I'll go with you." Meg folded her napkin, preparing to rise.

"No." Alexis's hand stopped her. "I'd rather you

didn't. This is sort of an exercise in trust and obedience. Your children must learn to do what I say, exactly as I say, and quickly. We can't afford to waste that time spent in looking to you for confirmation. It might never come down to that, but if it should a split second could make the difference in life or death." At Meg's stricken look Alexis squeezed her shoulder. "I'm sorry, I don't mean to frighten you."

Meg's lashes swept her cheeks, hiding her eyes for the briefest instant. "Frightened or not, I should understand so I don't interfere."

"Great." Alexis smiled at her. "Thank you."

Shiloh waited until Alexis and her charges were gone before he said softly. "She'll keep them safe."

"I know." Meg twisted her napkin into tortured knots.

"Just for a while her authority will supersede yours. She'll do it carefully and naturally. The children won't notice now, or when she fades out of the picture."

"She's cared for children at risk before?"

"Many times. She's the best at it."

"A strange vocation for a woman like her."

"Not strange at all," Shiloh contradicted. "Especially for a woman like Alexis. She loves children, and every child she can save is a payment on a debt that isn't hers."

Meg looked up, and her nervous hands were still. From Shiloh's tone she knew that there was more.

"When she was seventeen Alexis witnessed a kidnapping. She was traveling with her brother and his family in a Middle Eastern country. He was a minor diplomat. The hostages taken, a boy of eight and a girl of five, were his children. She was powerless to stop the abduction, but vowed she wouldn't be again. She made governessing her life, adding certain skills that made her unique.'' He didn't elaborate, leaving to Meg's common sense the details of the training Alexis had mastered. ''When a child is in jeopardy it's Alexis who's wanted.''

Meg turned to look out the window. Alexis and her charges sat by the pool. The blond woman was gesturing, setting the rules with a pleasant firmness. ''What became of the children?''

''They vanished. No amount of searching turned up a clue. The ransom demands were followed to the letter. The money was never picked up. They were just...gone.''

''Poor lost babies. Poor Alexis.''

''Good can come of evil. Alexis is that good.''

Meg watched her children with their devoted caretaker. ''I'm glad she's here for my children.''

''She'll protect them with her life.''

Meg nodded, believing, not turning her gaze from Alexis. ''When I first saw her, I thought she was beautiful, but I didn't know how beautiful.''

Shiloh folded Meg's hand in his. The profile he studied was framed by a mass of dark hair, not blond. His voice was deep and softly resonant as he murmured thoughtfully, ''Very beautiful.''

Four

"Yiee!" Tommy whooped, dismounted a broomstick christened Dakota and sprawled on the grass.

Meg looked up from her sketch, taking stock. Samantha slept by her on a toy-strewn quilt; the twins tumbled on the lawn with Alexis. Today their game was cowboys and Indians at the circus with Alexis as cowboy cum ringmaster.

They were comfortable at the inn. After a week it seemed they'd never known another home. Shiloh's security was unobtrusive; their lives continued with little disruption. There were rules and boundaries, but in a place this full of new discoveries no one noticed. Except for the ever-present specter of Ballenger this could be a restful vacation.

Ballenger! Meg couldn't forget him. At times she

managed to push him to the back of her thoughts, but he was there, waiting. Should she forget, her constant reminder was the magnificent Jeb Lattimer who faded in and out of the woodwork, but never for long. He stayed on the fringes, his handsome face calm, his searching eyes never still.

Meg stifled the impulse to wave at him as he bent over a newspaper he pretended to read. Instead she let her gaze travel over the people who gathered by the pool or in the garden café. Most were guests who had been coming to the inn for years. Some were not. These she had come to think of as Shiloh's army.

There were no strangers at the inn. Shiloh hadn't allowed it. Nor had he allowed their situation to be known. Thank God, any stories that reached this little Carolina hamlet hadn't included the photograph. Notoriety hadn't preceded them. Except to the special few, Meg was simply a widow on holiday with her children. For that she would be eternally grateful to Shiloh and his foresight. It allowed the children a natural interaction with the guests, restoring a sense of normalcy in their lives.

''Watch, Mom.'' Eddie's call was a trill of excitement, and Meg's spirits soared. Her quiet child rarely called attention to himself. With a flailing of arms and flying feet he executed a passable cartwheel, and another not so good. His bottom hit the grass with a thud as his shaky arms failed him.

''Ouch.'' Meg winced, forcing herself not to rush to him. She waited and worried. The wheezing sounds that rose from his sturdy little chest deepened, mounting in volume until Meg realized he was laughing.

"I bombed, Mom, but not until I'd done one!" He leaned back on his hands and lifted his face to the sky and crowed. "If I can do one, I can do another, wait and see."

"Yeah!" Tommy plopped unceremoniously beside him. "Then you can teach me."

Alexis looked up from the blade of grass she'd found so amazingly interesting, her gaze passed fondly over the boys. In her smile Meg read more than words. Meg wanted to laugh, to rejoice. Eddie had begun to step from his brother's shadow. Little by little he'd ventured out, accepting new challenges, risking failure. Once he wouldn't have tried the cartwheel and would never have laughed at his tumble.

"You're gonna have to teach me the first part, Eddie." Tommy stood offering his brother a hand. "I already know how to fall. I've done it already, lotsa times."

As they galloped away, heels kicking up like frisky colts, Meg felt no need to call a warning. A few bruises, a skinned knee or two would be well worth their cost. Neither child understood that Eddie had just taken a heavy weight off Tommy's five-year-old shoulders. Only Meg had seen the burden Eddie's timidness had been for his twin. Nobody had ever understood that a part of Tommy's assertiveness was bravado, that somewhere in his child's thoughts he believed he must have the courage of two. Nobody but her had seen or understood—except Alexis, and Shiloh.

The fragrance of the pine trees behind her filled her lungs. A breeze was warm on her skin. A·quail called; another answered. A hummingbird darted on invisible wings from one crimson flower to the next. The world and its troubles seemed an eon away. This was very nearly paradise, Meg decided, and she could stay forever.

"But Lawndale is our home," she chided herself firmly. "And to Lawndale we shall return." She wiped her damp palms on the legs of her faded jeans and shifted from her crossed-legged position. Tossing a pencil into her art bag she selected another. Her glance skimmed once more over her children before she put her foolish daydreams away and returned to her work.

She hadn't for a moment thought she would be able to concentrate on creating the latest adventure of Sonny and his shadow despite an imminent deadline. When she packed for the trip she included the tools of her profession from habit. The frayed bag with its sketch pad and colored pens and her notebook always went where she did.

Surprisingly, once they'd settled in and grown accustomed to the expected routines, work fairly flew from her fingers to the paper. The story seemed more exciting, her illustrations more vivid. She held up the half-finished sketch of two boys picking flowers in a field of clover and inspected it critically. It was true; she'd never worked so well.

"That's very good," a familiar voice commented.

Meg placed the drawing aside before she looked up into Shiloh's intriguing face. He hadn't changed from his morning ride. The rough clothes needed for his daily joust with Dakota suited him wonderfully. The closely woven shirt with its sleeves turned back over brawny arms clung to his body, rippling over his deep chest and flat stomach. The hip-hugging jeans, worn low and belted by a thin strip of unadorned leather, molded hard thighs and calves before they were drawn over serviceable boots.

He leaned lazily against the tree trunk, relaxed and comfortable. The taut, chill wariness was gone, his gaze was easy and warm as he smiled down at her.

A feeling of happiness set the easy pace of her heart into an uneven rush. She looked away, managing a demure acknowledgment of his compliment.

"You shouldn't let compliments embarrass you, Meg. Your work is more than good, as surely you know. If you don't then I'll have to tell you more often," he teased. His gaze moved to the subtle swell of her breasts rising in quick, telling breaths of blushing pride.

Beneath the sweeping veil of lashes his blue eyes lingered, darkening to midnight, and a ceaseless hunger smoldered beneath his mischief. It would be so easy to lean down to her, to set her long hair free from its clasp and let his fingers drift with it in a slow, whispering caress over her, discovering mysteries sweet and enticing.

Oh, God! Yes, it would be easy. So easy and so wrong.

Would it always be wrong for him? he wondered bleakly. Always the wrong time, the wrong place? *The wrong reason.* Shiloh's teeth clenched, and a muscle rippled in his jaw. He pushed away from the tree, destroying an illusion. He willed the sudden tension from his hard, lean body, forced the stony lines of his face into a smile. His voice was only a little rough as he gained firmer footing. "I see you've reached the point in your story when Shadow becomes a real little boy."

Meg was surprised he knew her work. As he knelt beside her she ventured, "Sonny's the courage, Shadow the wisdom."

"Like Tommy and Eddie."

"Yes." He truly understood.

"I've watched the children, and you."

"Then you know you were right." Meg laid a pen aside.

"About what?"

"You said the children would be happy."

"And their mother? Is she contented here?"

"I am. More than I have a right to be."

"Balderdash! You have every right to contentment and happiness. It's your inalienable right, written into the constitution of Stonebridge Inn." He hoped to make her smile with his nonsense, but the pensive expression did not alter.

"You've been kinder to me than I deserve."

"Why would you not deserve kindness, Meg?"

"There's a poor, hurt man out there who's been turned into a monster, wanting nothing more than to bring even more hurt to the world, and it's my fault." She unmercifully twisted the gold band on her right hand. "In my own weak way I'm responsible for what Keith did."

Shiloh felt a sense of helplessness as disturbing as her guilt. He wanted to challenge her demons but they were too obscure, of too little substance. How could he fight insanity and cowardice? How could he convince her that she owed nothing to Ballenger, a man who'd drifted beyond the bounds of reason long before the destruction of his family? How could he fight the weaknesses and subtle cruelties of a husband long dead?

I can't fight them, he thought. Not until I know what torments her. His gaze fell on the ring, her wedding ring, worn on her right hand. His answer lay in that gesture. Worn in sentiment or grief, it would be on the proper finger of the proper hand. Worn as it was, it was a symbol. A symbol of what?

He slid his hand beneath hers in an effort to stop the punishment she inflicted on herself. He was conscious of her bruises. His own damnable creations, done the day they arrived. "Meg." Shiloh touched her cheek with a fingertip, letting it glide to her chin, lifting her face. "You deserve to be happy. Before you leave, I'll prove it."

"You've already shown me that happiness can exist with guilt." Her gaze held his, and he saw in it that a small measure of her contentment survived.

"Then we've made a beginning." He squeezed her hand in encouragement and released it. His own hand felt suddenly empty and useless. To bridge an awkward gap his mind leaped to a comfortable subject. "Caroline sent her love. She meant to get by this week, but with an important piece of equipment down she was frantically busy."

"I thought I might ask her to dinner, if it's okay."

"You don't have to ask my permission to have someone for dinner, Meg. You're a guest, not a prisoner. You'll have to wait for Caroline, though. She and the boys left this morning to meet Gabe. They'll spend a few days together and bask in the sun of a tropical paradise."

"She misses him terribly, doesn't she?"

"Pete misses him almost as much."

"What are they like? Pete and Gabe, I mean?"

Shiloh settled down beside her, his back against the tree, his shoulders touching hers. He was quiet, composing his thoughts. Samantha stirred in her sleep and he smiled, flicking a leaf from her hair. Beyond them Eddie did an imitation of a whirling dervish to the tune of Alexis and Tommy's laughter. "Gabe was a wanderer. His work took him all over the world. It was exotic and exciting and almost got him killed. He came to the inn to recover from a sniper's attack. One look at Caroline and his wandering days were over. The most exciting place for Gabe is with her."

"How old was Pete?"

"He was thirteen and on his way to his first year at Stonebridge Academy."

''Did he resent Gabe?''

''Not for a minute. Pete's a carbon copy of his father. Mark was a generous man. He would have wanted Caroline to be happy. So did Pete. He loves Gabe, and he worships Shiloh Mark.''

''Shiloh Mark. They honor you with the name.''

''Mark and I were a part of Caroline's life long before Gabe. Mark was her childhood sweetheart. They were married only days before he went to Vietnam. He was the only nonvolunteer on our mission, the only one who didn't survive the prison camp. When it was finally ended, I came to offer Caroline a poor substitute for her husband—my condolences.

''I liked the country and the people. The inn was for sale so I decided to stay. I've done very little for Caroline except be her friend, but Gabe thinks differently. The baby's name was their way of remembering Pete's father and including me in their happiness.''

''Shiloh Mark Jackson. A beautiful name, a wonderful honor.'' Meg's voice was low, distracted, her thoughts filled with Shiloh. He spoke of Mark Donovan, and she heard pain for a life lost, for lives shattered by the loss. She understood, at last, the strong bond he shared with Caroline. One as deeply rooted in respect and admiration as honor and compassion. Shiloh had helped her rebuild her life, yet it was Gabe Caroline loved. ''Gabe Jackson,'' Meg mused thoughtfully. ''He must be quite a man.''

''He is. It takes quite a man for Caroline. Speaking

of Caroline, she sent you her love and a rare experience. She sent you Joe."

"Joe?"

"Joe," Shiloh said and maddeningly would make no further explanation. "Samantha's stirring; she should be awake in a minute. I'll round up the boys and speak to Alexis while you put away your supplies. Then I'll take you to meet him."

Meg didn't immediately gather up her material. Her gaze followed Shiloh instead. She watched, entranced by the long gliding stride, the sway of his heavy shoulders and the smile that moved like sunlight over his features. The chill that colored their every encounter was never evident when he was with the children. He attracted them like a magnet, and his pleasure in them was almost boyish. His laugh was deeper, more real. He was happier in their company than she'd ever seen him.

Now as he leaned over Alexis in earnest conversation, with Tommy clinging to one leg and Eddie to the other, Meg felt a little wistful. He had come to them as he had Caroline, but it was with the children he formed a special bond. He was their friend, the male influence they'd needed. Meg knew she should be forever grateful, but her happiness was tempered by a sense of loss.

"I'm acting like a fool. How can I lose what isn't mine?" she muttered without thinking what she'd said. "My children are safe and happier than they've ever been. I'll take one day at a time and not think of tomorrow." Tomorrow? Was that the sense of loss? Was she thinking of the future when they would leave Stonebridge? When they would leave Shiloh?

A cold hand seemed to close around her heart; her throat hurt from the crush of unchecked emotions. Her own words echoed in her mind. *How can I lose what isn't mine?* Dear heaven! What had happened to her?

"Nothing has happened!" The words exploded from her. She clutched at her sketch book to steady her hands. "Nothing!"

"Ma mad?" Samantha blinked owlishly, her skin flushed and dewy with sleep.

"Of course not, darling." Meg swept her into her lap, hugging her, drawing comfort from her tiny body and the tight grip of her chubby arms. She kissed each droopy eyelid and hugged her closer. "I was thinking how glad I am that you're my own special little girl."

"Sam special." Samantha latched on to a new thought and explored it.

"Yes, you are."

"TomEddie special." She joined their names as she always had.

"Certainly, and even more special because they have you for a sister."

"Lexis special."

"Alexis is a special lady."

"Lo Lo special." Samantha finished with a flourish.

Meg lifted her head from her child's bright hair, and her eyes found Shiloh. He had dismissed Alexis, as he often did, giving her a break from her duties. Hand in hand he walked with the boys, back to the shade of her pine. ''Yes,'' she agreed in a half whisper. ''He's very special.''

''Mom,'' Tommy called excitedly. ''Shiloh has a new friend for us.''

''His name is Joe,'' Eddie chimed in.

''So I've heard.'' Meg laughed, her troubled thoughts no match for their enthusiasm.

''I'll take this sweetheart from you and we'll go meet him.'' Shiloh lifted Samantha into the air as she giggled and kicked. Then settling her in one arm he offered Meg his hand. ''Come on, lazybones, Joe's waiting.''

They walked across the lawn, Meg's bag bouncing against Eddie's leg as he skipped in Tommy's wake. Samantha chattered to herself in Shiloh's arms. They made a handsome picture. Shiloh sensed as much as saw the guests watching, speculating. He could almost hear the silent applause of the inveterate matchmakers who had been on his case for what seemed like forever. Wickedly he put his arm around Meg, his hand curving around her shoulder, drawing her against him. The imaginary applause grew thunderous.

She fit nicely in the shelter of his arm, their steps synchronized naturally in cadence. He guided her past the garden, avoiding the veranda and its occupants, taking them to the private stair that led to his apartment. He didn't stop to wonder why he shunned the easy camaraderie of his guests. He was conscious only of the heat of her skin beneath the cotton of her shirt, the clean tantalizing scent of her hair, the fullness of her breasts.

For a week he'd stayed at a distance, keeping their involvement on a friendly, controlled dimension. Today he'd ventured into dangerous waters and discovered his restraint had been worthless, his power over desire a farce.

"Will Joe come to the door if I ring the bell?" Tommy called from the top of the stair.

Shiloh was jolted from his thoughts. "No!" he shouted. "Don't ring the bell."

"Oh." Tommy backed away from the railing, his bottom lip quivering.

Shiloh stopped at the foot of the stair, disturbed by his harsh command. Sliding his arm from Meg he handed Samantha to her and climbed to Tommy. At the landing he knelt by the boy. "I didn't mean to shout. I was thinking about something else and... never mind. It doesn't matter what I was thinking; I shouldn't have yelled at you. But you mustn't ever ring the bell while Joe is here; he hates doorbells. Okay?"

"Okay." Tommy accepted Shiloh's hug.

"What does he do if the bell rings?" Eddie asked.

"He says words your mom wouldn't want you to know."

"Like what?" Tommy wanted to know.

"Don't ask; take my word for it."

Hello.

The raspy voice ended their conversation.

"Is that Joe?" Tommy whispered, awed by the deafening volume of the cry.

Speak up! Speak up!

The voice lost its gruffness, growing louder as it rose an octave on each command.

"Is he an old man?" Eddie wondered.

"Yes and no," Shiloh said.

Come in. Come in. See poor lonesome Joe.

The voice was weak and trembling, breaking pitifully on each long, drawn adjective.

"He sure sounds like an old man. Is he sick?" Tommy frowned.

"He's very old, but he's not sick, and he's definitely not a man."

"Whatever he is, he sounds terribly lonesome." Meg had finished the steps and stood by him. Her mischievous grin proved that she knew exactly what was beyond the door. "If he won't hurt the children, why don't we go in and visit?"

"He won't." Shiloh turned the lock and stepped aside.

"A parrot," Tommy cried. "A real one."

"Joe doesn't consider himself a bird. He was part of Mark's family for nearly forty years. He's Pete's now."

"Jingo bird." Samantha struggled out of Meg's arms.

"No, honey," Shiloh said as he walked her to the cage. "He's sorta big for a hummingbird."

"Jingo bird." Samantha was adamant in her decision.

Meg chuckled, saying, ''Obviously it's not just the hummingbird that reminds her of Jingo's helicopter. I guess Joe's Jingo bird until she decides differently.''

''Joe won't mind,'' Shiloh said. ''Would you like to sit down while they all get acquainted?''

''No, thanks, I've been sitting all morning. It looks like we might be here awhile, though. They're in a Mexican standoff.'' Meg indicated the children, locked in a stare with the brilliantly plumed parrot.

''That's Joe's macho act. He's a soft touch for kids.''

''You credit him with a lot of intelligence.''

''You should hear Gabe on the subject.''

Joe began to croon, his gnarled claws and yellow legs shifting from one end of his perch to another. His stubby green body swayed, and his saffron head ducked in time with his song. He stopped to preen a scarlet-splashed wing. A translucent lid dropped over one eye, and a sound like a chuckle began in his throat.

''He likes us,'' Tommy cried. ''He winked and laughed.''

''What's not to like about you?'' Shiloh asked.

Shut up and kiss the broad.

The cry was a thin, ear-splitting shriek straight out of a jungle night.

''Joe,'' Shiloh scolded. ''Mind your manners.''

Kiss the broad.

The air vibrated with the call. Joe resumed his dance, his abbreviated body moving in a vaudeville strut.

"Why don't you just kiss Mom like he said, and he'll be quiet," Eddie suggested with his fingers in his ears, his exasperation indicating how obtuse grown-ups could be.

"Yeah, Shiloh, if you'd just kiss her Joe would stop hurting our ears and he wouldn't break his neck falling off his perch." If Tommy was any less impatient he hid it well.

"Tommy! Eddie!" Meg didn't know if she should laugh, or scold them for their impudence.

"They do have a point," Shiloh murmured in her ear.

"You know as well as I that stupid—" A growl from the cage cut her short. "That *bird* doesn't know what he's saying," she finished determinedly.

"He knows." Shiloh's hand rested lightly at her waist, its subtle pressure bringing her nearer. Mischief glinted in his eyes. "He knows exactly what he's doing. We mustn't hurt his feelings, must we?" Slowly, he leaned toward her, his lips brushing hers playfully.

The children's gleeful approval, even Joe's raucous cheer, were distant echoes in Meg ears. Her lips tingled from the fleeting caress; her head spun. Her legs bent like a marionette's, and only Shiloh kept her from falling.

"Ah. What price the silence?" His hand beneath her chin lifted her gaze to his. "One kiss." His voice was light, teasing. Laughter seemed to bubble beneath the surface. There was an engaging attractiveness that not even the scar and its ugly memories could mar.

This Shiloh was even more breathtaking than all

the others. Meg wished she could lift the weight of his burdens from his shoulders and banish the somber lines of worry from his face forever.

A kiss like wine.

The guttural growl was an inescapable reminder of time and circumstance. Meg had to distance herself from these feelings. Her laugh was a little hoarse as she slipped into the role she must play. ''Did you teach him that trick?''

''No, but I'm grateful to the person who did.''

''Are you?''

''Eternally.'' His tone altered. His laughter disappeared. His fingers splayed possessively over her back, their tips caressing her through her blouse. His eyes were the cool blue of a Nordic sky. The silver fire of moonbeams sparkled in them, but there was nothing cold in the gaze that studied her. ''I've wanted to kiss you from the very first time I saw you.''

''You have?''

''Uh-huh.'' His fingers stroked away a strand of dark hair; his palms framed her face. ''For three years I wondered what it would be like to hold you and kiss you. This week I've lain awake knowing only a hallway separated us. Less than a dozen steps that I hadn't the courage to take.''

''I can't believe you've ever lacked courage.'' Meg hesitated, unsure this studied seriousness was part of the game.

''This was different.''

''Why?''

''Because the woman I wanted was you.''

Samantha burbled to Eddie about the Jingo bird, and Tommy whooped. Meg struggled, trying desperately to remember they were here, that this was a game. Forcing a parody of a chuckle she said, ''So you bribed Caroline for the use of her bird.''

''Something like that.'' The beginning of a smile touched his mouth. ''For once Joe earned his room and board.''

''If he hadn't?''

''Then I would've fed him to Dakota,'' he said without batting an eye.

Choked laughter erupted from Meg. ''You wouldn't!''

''Couldn't, you mean,'' Shiloh drawled, sliding his arm around her again, drawing her back to his side. ''That Portugee bird and my badlands stallion have the strangest friendship this side of the zoo.''

''Don't tell me Joe rides Dakota.''

''All right, I won't.''

''But he does.'' Profoundly grateful for the return of his unpredictable humor she deliberately assumed the roll of straight man.

''He loves it.''

Meg sighed and changed the subject. ''Why do you call him Portugee?''

''Because he swears beautifully in Portuguese.''

''I see.'' Meg felt laughter rippling inside her like a mountain spring. His lunacy was as contagious as it was rare. ''Another question.''

''Ask.''

"Does he ride bareback or with a saddle?"

"Joe hates bareback." Shiloh glanced at his watch. "Which reminds me. I have to saddle Dakota in a few minutes."

"You bribed Joe to do his kiss routine with a ride!"

"Exactly."

"Shiloh!" Impulsively Meg flung her arms around him. "You're so good for us. For me. I can't remember when I've laughed, or been so foolish, or felt so free and safe."

"There's nothing I want more than to see you happy, Meg." He kissed her hair, keeping its fragrance with him.

Meg stepped from his embrace, her face lit by the happiness of their nonsensical banter. Her gaze searched his face, touching every gentle feature. "I can never thank you for what you've done."

"Shh. I don't want your gratitude." With his thumb he stroked the corner of her mouth, watching as her lips parted, revealing the white gleam of her even teeth, the pale rose of her tongue. He trembled with the knowledge that in this moment her mouth and its intoxicating depths were his for the taking.

She was vulnerable and trusting, unconsciously offering the first of many gifts. And he was human. He felt an ancient triumph, reveled in a masculine prowess as primordial as creation. He savored the sweet ache of desire. He wanted Meg Sullivan, but gratitude was not enough. For once in his life he wanted more from a woman than favors for favors given.

Suddenly his life seemed tawdry and empty. Nothing in it had taught him how to deal with such a woman. She had much to give, while he had nothing. Only his protection. With a low, despairing groan he gathered her roughly to him. "I'll keep you safe, Meg. I think I'd die if I didn't."

His hand was in her loosened hair. Shiloh, who still hurt from the loss of a friend so many years ago, was hurting now. "You won't fail us," she said, accepting the reversal of roles. "You couldn't."

She waited. Holding him, letting him hold her. After a bit his fingers untangled from her hair. His arms folded around her, keeping her as tenderly as he might Samantha. "What is it you do to me?" he muttered. "Are you woman, or siren sent to bewitch me?"

"Before this is done you'll think I'm a troublesome witch." Meg dropped her voice to a teasing tone, watching as his features relaxed.

"I don't see any warts." This after a prolonged study of her nose.

"I hide them."

"Oh, Lord! You're beginning to jabber like Caroline."

"I'll take that as a compliment."

"It was meant as one."

"Shiloh!" The shout barely preceded a knock at the door.

Shiloh stared down at her, his face filled with regret at the interruption. "The world intrudes," he said. Leaning forward, he kissed her, his lips brushing hers.

Abruptly he turned away. When he opened the door Jeb Lattimer was there with Alexis a pace behind.

"Ballenger's been spotted," the bearded giant said without preamble. His warm, amber eyes looked beyond Shiloh to Meg. There was sympathy in them. "I'm sorry, Meg. It looks like he's coming this way."

In a tick of the clock Meg's safe, enchanted world came crashing down around her.

Five

Meg sat alone at her table, tucked into a secluded corner, apart from the quiet activity of the dining room. She felt drawn and graceless, far too weary to join the gathering of congenial diners. Ironically it was that very weariness that had brought her here. Weariness and a disquieting need to catch even a glimpse of Shiloh.

Alexis had insisted Meg take a break from the confinement imposed by the sighting of Ballenger. Facing resistance, she bluntly observed that Meg's masquerade of serenity had begun to erode, causing concern in the children. In further persuasion the governess suggested all would profit from a break in unrelenting togetherness. ''Retreat, renew your strength, for the children,'' Alexis concluded her argument, and Meg capitulated.

Now, in the flickering shadows, Meg sat silently in the muted hum of easy conversations, toying with a dinner she didn't want. The chef's sumptuous dishes tasted like cardboard as she struggled to avoid the subjects foremost in her mind. It was a useless effort. She couldn't banish thoughts of the cunning madman who had destroyed her life once. Whose dementia had sent her on a journey to sanctuary and drawn people to her who had changed her forever.

Staring into her wineglass as if it were a crystal ball, she let herself question why she needed so much to see Shiloh's dark, scarred face and feel the touch of his gentle hands. She wondered if she would always feel lost without him.

''May I join you?''

The soft-spoken request drew her from the morass of perplexing questions and elusive answers. The deep voice was younger, the maturity not as rich, the edge of bitterness not yet eased by time. It was a beautiful voice, but not Shiloh's voice.

Turning from her study of the swirling, shimmering wine, and abandoning the futile pondering of her own mysterious heart, Meg looked up into Jeb Lattimer's smiling face and was grateful for the distraction.

For the first time Meg realized she had never really *seen* Jeb Lattimer. He was a necessary fixture in her life, a very real part of a life-or-death struggle, but she had never looked at Jeb the man. Not once had she considered what lay beneath the handsome face framed by flowing golden hair, nor appreciated the indomitable heart beating within his massive chest with a fierce loyalty to Shiloh, and her family. Self-absorbed and bemused, she hadn't looked into his amber eyes or detected the glint of humor sparkling in them.

Jeb waited, self-possessed and unruffled by her seemingly vacant stare. As silence stretched between them he said without animosity, "I didn't mean to interfere with your dinner." He glanced briefly at her barely touched food. "You looked as if you needed someone to talk to. If you'd rather not…"

A rare intrusion, now he was backing diplomatically away. She touched his sleeve. "Stay. Please. I could use some company."

Jeb set down his wineglass and slid into a seat with the grace of one accustomed to fitting a large body into small places. He should've dwarfed the chair but he was so at ease with his size that he neither overwhelmed nor intimidated. As she watched him over the table, Meg realized he was a comfortable man. Comfortable within himself, and comfortable to be with. That he was a man with a past was written on the bold features of his classically handsome face. He bore the mark of troubles. Like Shiloh, Jeb had walked through the valley of some private hell to become the man he was.

Shiloh! As she looked into Jeb's warm, amber eyes, she imagined her mind as a maze, with all paths leading to the enigmatic man who held the lives of all she loved in his hands.

''It would help if you could eat some of that.'' Jeb indicated the lobster salad before her. ''The chef won't be fooled by the way you've rearranged it.''

''Poor man, he's tried to tempt my appetite. It's always the same. I go through the motions, telling myself nothing's really changed, that Ballenger isn't really out there. It never works, still I try. Without some pretense, I'd lose my mind.''

''What you do, you do for the children, Meg.''

''I've used every crutch and device I could think of. If I smoked, now is when I think I'd need a cigarette.''

''You could smoke like a chimney and it wouldn't help,'' Jeb remarked practically, watching the downcast features beneath the mass of ebony hair.

''You're right. A cigarette is a poor substitute for courage.''

''You don't need substitutes. You have enough of the real thing. Perhaps too much for your own good.'' Jeb laced his fingers together and rested his hands on the table. ''Now,'' he said, ''why don't you tell me what's bothering you tonight.''

Meg stifled a sigh. He had let her ramble, guiding her slowly to the heart of her worries. Gathering her thoughts, she stared through the falling twilight, remembering that beyond these walls was a peace that Jeb guarded without disturbing it. Jeb, a man so different from Shiloh but cut from the same cloth. A mystery with hair of gold, not darkest black. Discreet, dedicated, unfathomable, ever-present and tireless. Did he sleep? Did Shiloh?

"Meg," Jeb prompted.

Reluctantly she turned toward him, shrugging dispiritedly. "There's been no more on Ballenger. He was seen at an airport in Georgia. Then he vanished. How can that happen?"

"The man's a chameleon. He has to be, considering how elusive he's been." Jeb clasped her wrist, reassuring. "This was a disappointment, but not the end of it."

"I understand how difficult this is for all of you. I know how hard you're working. The guard has been doubled. We aren't prisoners, but we're watched more closely. The children haven't noticed. Everyone's been very careful of that." Then softly, "Shiloh's worked around the clock for the past three days. Butler Enterprises...the investigation...I've hardly seen him."

"He won't stop until the man is behind bars, and you're safe. You have my word on it. Promises don't always seem like much, but I hope it helps some."

Meg nodded. "It helps. It reminds me that clouds do have silver linings. I never dreamed there could be friends like you and Alexis. Like Shiloh."

Leaning back in his seat, Jeb picked up his glass, a curious look crossing his face. Meg felt the critical study of eyes that gleamed like topaz over the rim of fragile crystal. Jeb's head tilted slightly as if he listened more to her tone than the recounting of unexpected gifts. With the smallest of smiles he carefully set the glass aside. "Shiloh had an unavoidable errand in the village, or he would be here."

"I know the inn can be protected like a fortress and that venturing beyond the grounds would deplete the manpower, but I wish I could see the village." She wanted to walk the wandering streets, tracing the paths Shiloh walked, immersing herself in the peace of Stonebridge, his refuge. She couldn't. She'd given her word never to leave the grounds. Not alone.

"Shiloh loves Stonebridge so much." His name on her tongue softened the regret in her face, and something new was in her eyes. "He's such a complex man, so reserved. I had no idea he was an artisan until he said something about his forge."

"Shiloh calls himself a blacksmith, not an artist," Jeb commented dryly.

"He's more than that."

"Of course he is," Jeb agreed. Then with a golden twinkle in his eye he teased, "Aren't you just as sure that he's responsible for hanging the stars and the moon?"

For a moment Meg was taken by surprise by this droll humor coming from this bear of a man. Then she realized the austere lines of his face had been softened by a smile. The mischievous twinkle she'd seen earlier was only the tip of the iceberg. Somewhere in his trial by fire Jeb had learned to treat the world with humor. Perhaps, with the troubles he encountered in his work, it was his defense against cynicism. As he sat smiling, with his overlong hair brushing his collar and the improbable bit of silken fleece on his chin, he looked less like the dangerous defender she intuitively knew he would be than an elegantly overgrown musketeer inviting the world to laugh with him.

"If that's masculine subtlety asking if I'm grateful for all Shiloh's done, the answer is yes, Jeb." Meg tossed him a mock glare, then, as her wily inquisitor lifted exaggeratedly innocent brows, she rushed on. "I wish I could watch him work."

"Oh." Jeb's smile seemed to be giving him trouble. "I strongly suspect you will."

"No. When this is over..." Her voice faded.

"It will be. Ballenger won't get as far as the inn. Shiloh won't give him the chance."

"I know." She tried to relax. "We couldn't be in better hands. It's still hard to believe he would jeopardize his own life to help perfect strangers."

"You were Keith's wife, not a stranger, and you'd met."

"I don't remember. How could I not remember Shiloh?"

Jeb lost his battle with his grin, and it spread in devilish delight over his face. Meg could see that he was mightily pleased with something. As if he alone possessed a secret. Before she could ask what, he sobered. "Grief consumes. As survivors we feel guilt, and living becomes such a chore we're blind to all but our own insular world."

The humor was gone. There was an unintentional note of grief and even anger in the words. The unresigned bitterness she'd heard earlier from one not quite old enough to keep it well hidden. "You speak from experience, don't you, Jeb?"

He was silent, his eyes closed. Meg regretted the question. He'd come offering company and conversation, and she'd repaid him by knocking at a door he wanted kept firmly closed. She wished she could retract the question and bring back his smile.

"Perhaps it's time," Jeb muttered. "Past time." He lifted his glass, draining it. When he spoke there was an uneven rhythm in his words. "There was a girl. Once. She was warm, intelligent, with a wonderful life ahead of her. God! She was so lovely it made your heart sing just to look at her. Laura," he said softly. "Her name was Laura. She was sixteen when she died."

"An accident?"

"No."

Meg touched his clenched hands with hers. The weight that had been gathering in her chest grew heavier. "You loved her."

"From the day she was born and I was ten years old. When we were children our families thought our attachment was charming. Later the age difference was considered too great. I agreed. I withdrew from her. To give her time to grow up, to enjoy being a teenager, to know her own mind. She didn't understand. She thought I was deserting her."

A hard shudder shook his massive frame. He drew a long breath, releasing it slowly. "I didn't see...not until it was too late. Her parents and mine blamed me. For a long time I believed them and closed myself off in my own corner of hell. I don't remember a lot about those days. Perhaps it's a blessing."

Jeb seemed distant, unfocused. Meg offered no comment. There was none she could make. Her hand tightened over his, waiting for him to continue.

"Is it really so important that you remember Shiloh and the funeral?"

With that the subject of Laura was closed. Meg suspected forever. He had opened a very private grief, establishing a common bond, so that he might help her. Meg almost wept at the magnitude of what he offered. Instead, she followed him to safer ground. Leaning back in her seat she pushed her plate away. "I'm not trying to remember so much as I need to understand. He's done so much for my family, and for Caroline's before me. I need to know why he's taken us as his special burden."

"You aren't a burden. He felt responsible for the survival of his men in the prison. As a civilian he helps now when he's needed. All who've stayed in contact do."

"Have others drifted away like Keith?"

"A few. Most feel a bond with Shiloh that defies distance or difference. If there's trouble, help's there for the asking." A shrug and a pause let Meg fill the blanks. "The feeling's mutual. Not one would hesitate if Shiloh needed him."

"I had no idea he existed. I couldn't have asked for help, and I doubt Caroline did."

"No," Jeb conceded. "Caroline asked for nothing."

"Then why?"

"Meg, Shiloh might look like a fallen angel but

he's one of the world's few truly kind men. He can be as brutal as needed in his business, but that's a Shiloh separate from this. The man you know came to Caroline out of respect for Mark, not to be the martyr. There was regret, too, for Mark was the one man under his command who'd died in the prison."

So this was the bond that Meg had sensed between Shiloh and Caroline. A common loss, a friend, a husband. It explained much. The deep friendship, the loving without becoming lovers.

Sounds from nearby tables drifted by. Silver was an elegant chime against china, laughter trailed a low comment. Chairs slipped in whispers over carpet. Like an eddying stream they filled a hush.

Meg roused herself from her thoughts. "You sound as if you were there with them."

"Do I?" Jeb smiled slightly as he shook his head. "I was too young for Vietnam. Shiloh and I met shortly after his return. I was an uprooted rich kid, disowned by family and struggling to make a go of a security service. He trusted me with a small chore and was pleased with the results. That was our beginning."

"He told you about Mark and Keith?"

"Very little. Most of what I know came from Caroline."

Meg sighed faintly. "When I first saw him I wondered what kind of man he was. I couldn't believe he was for real."

"Do you have any doubts now?"

"None."

"Shiloh came to you because he cares. It's that simple."

"How did he know about Evan Ballenger? The story was over all the local papers, but they would hardly reach this far."

"You're forgetting Butler Enterprises is based in Atlanta, which is near enough to Lawndale that the papers would carry the stories. Before that, through a network his men share, he learned of the drinking. But it was too late. When Keith was killed he came to mourn. It was all he could do without intruding. I don't suppose it's occurred to you.... No." He shook his head. "Of course, it hasn't. It's too soon."

"Too soon for what?"

"Nothing." Meg's question was dismissed with a wave of a hand. She could see Jeb had no intention of sharing with her the rest of his observation. "I was rambling, thinking how closely sympathy resembles other emotions. Guilt, shame, hate, love."

"Pity?"

"No. Not pity. Never from Shiloh. He's had too much himself. You were alone, you needed someone. Shiloh decided he was that someone. Whatever the reason, it isn't pity. Any further explanation will have to come from Shiloh.

"Now—" he laughed as he lifted his glass, then realizing it was empty set it down. "I'll climb off my soapbox as gracefully as I can and I promise I won't sermonize anymore for the rest of the evening." Normally a man of few words, Jeb decided he'd said quite enough for one night. He wouldn't speak of the picture Shiloh had carried with him for three years. Nor would he tell of the wild, angry frenzy precipitated by Ballenger's threat, or the cold, frightening rage it spawned. Only Shiloh could tell her of that, and how deeply he cared.

"You're looking rather pleased with yourself. I think I see feathers on your lips," Meg observed with an effort to put both their sadnesses away.

"I had steak for dinner, not bird."

"Maybe so, but you've been grinning like the proverbial cat who got the proverbial canary."

"Was I?'

"You don't intend to share the joke?"

"No, and it's not a joke."

"If you insist," Meg said. It had just began to register how strange the entire conversation had been. Until this evening, Jeb had been courteous and pleasant but totally professional. Tonight he had deliberately stepped out of character. Perhaps, she thought, he'd revealed his true character, and in the course of his revelation had discovered something. Something in her conversation, hidden in its nuances. It had not disappointed him.

She had made discoveries of her own. She was beginning to understand Shiloh's intense sense of responsibility and the equally intense loyalties he inspired. Jingo might suffer from a case of hero worship, but Jeb spoke of Shiloh as a respected and treasured friend. She hadn't known before now how good it was to have such friends.

Running her hand beneath her hair, massaging the

tired muscles of her neck, she commented, "I feel as if I've been on an emotional roller-coaster."

"The right roller coaster can be fun." With no trace of a smile he switched subjects. "How are the children and Joe?"

"Joe's a godsend. Because of him the children haven't noticed how closely Alexis and I have watched them. They love that crazy bird. They sleep with him in their room, they eat with him. They aren't here tonight because nobody wanted to leave Joe. They'll miss him when Caroline takes him back."

"Ask her to let him stay."

"Would she?"

"I'm sure of it. Joe loves children and he's lonely now that Pete is away at school and Shiloh Mark is too young to play." He paused. "Speaking of Shiloh Mark, his godfather is here."

Meg's smile slipped. Mechanically she turned, her head moving as if it were only delicately balanced on her neck. Her loose hair slipped strand by strand over her shoulder like a languidly opened fan. Her breast rose raggedly, straining against her blouse. The air seemed thin, inadequate. Her skin grew clammy; her cheeks flamed. The only sound was the susurrant rush of her heart.

He filled the foyer with his particular blend of brawny slenderness. His hair was disheveled, his clothing rumpled. The stubble of his beard was a deep shadow over cheeks and jaw. Shallow creases lining his forehead had become furrows, and the scar that rent his beautiful eye was a livid stain against the chalk of his face.

Meg knew he must be beyond exhaustion. Yet he was here, lacking a certain sartorial splendor, but as enduring as stone. His strength might falter but it would never desert him. He bore the weight of trouble at his cost. Perhaps someday a woman, small, fragile, but infinitely precious, would be allowed to share his life and would contain that strength with love.

As she stared at him, her mouth yearning for his, Meg wanted to be that woman. More than she wanted anything.

"Dammit!" Jeb grumbled. "Look at this summer's airhead. From the day Shiloh hired her she's complained."

The young hostess, the target of Jeb's disgust, was speaking earnestly as Shiloh's tired eyes probed the candlelit darkness. "Do the best you can," he muttered tersely, longing for the day Julie Townsend would end her summer sabbatical. Stepping past the woman he forgot her as he found their secluded table.

"He's worn out." Meg's cry was intended for Jeb, but in distress her voice carried beyond him.

"That sounds like an accusation," Shiloh said with a thin smile.

"I'm sorry, I didn't mean it to."

"It takes more than a few days of concentrated effort to wear me down."

"Your eye hurts, doesn't it?" Meg's worried inspection moved over his face.

Shiloh didn't look at her. He couldn't, for she was

right. He was worse than tired. His guard was down. Meg might read in him more than he dared allow. Pointedly he changed the subject. ''Any problems since I left for the village, Jeb?''

''None. We have a reprieve. Forget the investigation for a while and rest. We both know Meg's right. You're tired, and your eye does hurt.''

Shiloh shot him a look asking what in hell he thought he was doing, but it was met by an innocent expression.

''Please sit down, Shiloh,'' Meg said quietly.

He drew out a chair. As he sank into it he knew the light from a guttering candle must cast haggard shadows on his face, deepening the lines with darkness. Unflattering, perhaps, but he was grateful he need only contend with candlelight. His eye had become a shrieking torment, and he longed to shield it from even this bit of brightness. He would not. He had seen a look of pity on her face before. No more.

Old friends like Jeb might bully him into resting. Understanding that, though some perversity in him fought it, rest was the best medicine for his pain. They might deplore his stubbornness, calling him mulish or seven kinds of an obstinate fool, but none pitied or took public notice of his anguish.

Looking into Jeb's guileless face Shiloh wondered what mischievous purpose his unusual goading served. ''Don't you have somewhere to go, Jeb? Something to do?''

''Not a thing. It's rare I have such a lovely dinner companion so I'm making the most of it.''

"How?" Shiloh growled in a sudden burst of jealousy.

"We've had a very interesting conversation."

"What about?"

"Nothing you'd be interested in."

"Wouldn't I?" One brow moved, the other didn't.

"We were discussing cats and canaries."

"You don't like cats, Jeb."

"Don't have to like cats to talk about cats." Jeb shrugged.

"Before I brought you to Stonebridge you were a sensible man. Now I think you've been around our red-haired friend too long."

Meg laughed with them, but heard a jarring note in Shiloh's laughter. There was a ragged thread in the deep, mellow tone. The curve of his lips was a little too tense, the line of his throat too strained. Suddenly she knew. Only Shiloh's rigid discipline contained a cry of pain.

She ached to comfort him. The emptiness of her leaden arms raised its own silent cry, one that would go unanswered. Lessons hard learned, in her home, at the helicopter pad, marked her heart as bruises had her fingers. Yet it was not fear of rejection that kept her hands folded primly in her lap. She would risk any injury for him. What she couldn't risk was adding to his distress.

Twice before he had taken her concern, not for compassion, but for pity. The sort he abhorred. Unctuous pity that brought a haunted, lost look to his face. Even though her desire to hold him, to draw his head to her breast and stroke away his suffering was her own torment, she would deny herself for Shiloh's sake. Instead, wisely, she laughed, making no acknowledgment of the truth beneath their teasing.

In a lightning switch Jeb said on a hunch, "There's been news of Ballenger."

"Yes." Shiloh's expression was closed. "It came just now, as I returned from the village."

"He slipped away?" Meg knew the news would be bad. Shiloh's weariness was too complete for anything else.

"It was never Ballenger at all."

"Never!" Meg's confusion was total.

"The man was a low-life Lothario dodging a subpoena in a child-support case. Dammit!" Anger erupted in Shiloh. "If he hadn't run, we could've saved precious hours, avoided wasted effort." His hand became a fist of weathered leather against the white of the tablecloth, and his weariness compounded.

"How can it be worse that this wasn't Ballenger at all?" Meg asked, hating to natter at him.

"If it had been our man," he told her, "even if he escaped, we'd have an idea where to begin our search."

"I see." Meg had to look away. His bitter sense of failure was too much to bear.

"It was too obvious, out of character. Ballenger would never show himself that openly. Dammit!" Jeb blurted. "Another delay."

"One of many," Shiloh said wearily.

Meg looked from one man to the other. ''So,'' she asked after a moment. ''Where does that leave us?''

''Exactly nowhere,'' Shiloh said gruffly. ''Preliminary reports indicate the man is a genius, as wily as he is cunning. He's like smoke, leaving no trace. He could be in California, or Lawndale.''

''Or Stonebridge,'' Meg added, her voice almost failing.

Shiloh touched her shoulder. His gaze met hers fully for the first time, the pain and desire in them banked to a deep, smoldering glitter. ''He isn't here.''

Not yet. The words hovered between them. A silent warning, a sepulchral breath coiling through darkening minds, loosing a numbing terror. The room once so pleasant, its welcoming loveliness warmed by the flickering of a multitude of flames, was suddenly frigid, chilling Meg to the marrow. Only Shiloh's hand at her shoulder comforted her, staving off the threat of that cold voice. She wanted to go into his arms, surrounding herself with his assurance.

''Meg, listen to me.'' His words were distinct, each a separate entity, forcing her to comprehend. ''We have no reason to believe he could stumble across our trail. Our flight plan and the charter were filed, but they were then sealed by special order. Only Jingo knows them and he'd die before he would say anything.''

Like a parent coping with the misgivings of a frightened child, he spelled it out again for her, in verbal black and white, leaving no gray areas of doubt. ''Genius, or madman, or ghost, Ballenger has no way to connect you with me or with this place.''

''Of course he couldn't.'' Jeb was as definite as Shiloh. ''If he should, do you think he'd manage to slip by our militia? Good Lord! Half of them would be more at home in a Latin American jungle with machine guns and machetes. If our ghost managed to get by them, he'd have to be a certified idiot to challenge either Shiloh or me. Ballenger's not a big man. Hell, I look like a grizzly compared to him. And pound for pound, Shiloh would take him apart.''

Meg shivered. The picture Jeb painted was not as encouraging as intended. She couldn't forget that Ballenger had the inhuman strength of madness in his favor. Dutifully she attempted a laugh, succeeding with only a miserable croak. ''You're right. I'm crediting him with a sort of evil power.''

Out of the darkness the hostess appeared at Shiloh's shoulder. ''Mr. Butler, you have a call. The gentleman said it had nothing to do with the current trouble, but it is important.''

''Thank you.'' Shiloh dismissed her. Carl Simmons had drawn phone duty. The summons was unlike him. Something was wrong.

''Are you sure it isn't him?'' Suddenly Meg didn't know if she wanted the reprieve to continue or if the greatest relief would be to end the waiting.

''It isn't Ballenger,'' Shiloh assured. The hand resting on her shoulder slid to her neck, kneading with persuasive gentleness the knotted muscles. ''We don't know where he is, but we know he isn't here.'' His hand trailed down her arm to her hand. His clasp was firm. ''My call's waiting.''

She looked up from their joined hands. Her smile was less tentative, color that fled her cheeks began to return. ''I'll be fine, Shiloh.''

''Yes.'' Tenderness ran like a satin ribbon through the rough timbre of his voice. All he'd meant to hide was in his face. Only the torpid armor of false calm she'd drawn around herself blinded Meg to the truth. He stared down at her, wanting to slide his fingers into that shimmering hair, to bury his face in it, breathing its scent of jasmine and roses. He wanted to lose himself in her. Forgetting hate and revenge. Forgetting Ballenger.

Ballenger. Shiloh sighed, released her hand and turned to Jeb. ''This shouldn't take long.''

''I'll be here.''

Shiloh nodded and stood. ''Try not to worry. I'll be back as soon as I can.''

Without him the room was empty and lackluster. The tables were sparsely populated, most of the diners having hurried to their games of bridge or chess or to that good book. Later there would be time for a late-night snack or nightcap.

Jeb waited as he'd promised, but he had grown tense and watchful.

Meg touched his arm. ''What is it?''

''I don't know.'' He shook his head. ''A hunch, a premonition. Like that cold spot you feel when a gun is trained on you. You don't see it, but you know it's there, and you wait for the bullet.'' He fell silent. It was a moment before Meg realized Shiloh was approaching their table, his face a flinty mask.

Meg started from her chair, reaching out to him. ''Are you all right?''

''Gabe's been hurt.''

''How? What happened?'' Meg cried.

''How bad?'' Jeb added.

''His plane crashed on takeoff. He's alive, but it's not certain how serious his injuries are. Caroline and the boys were booked on a later flight.''

Meg swayed against Shiloh. His arms were around her, holding her against him. He lowered her to her chair, taking her hands in his. ''His leg is broken and he has a concussion. We know that much.''

''The hospital on that island is better than average,'' Jeb said.

''Is it equipped to deal with a shattered leg and a head injury in a man who's had another serious injury in the recent past?''

Jeb slid back his chair. ''I'll find out.''

Shiloh didn't look away from Meg. ''I'll be there as soon as I take Meg to her room.''

Meg barely noticed Jeb depart. ''When will you leave?''

''I'm not.'' His breath caressed her cheek.

''But Caroline…'' With her heart in her throat she stared into that wonderful, wounded face, waiting for him to make everything all right.

''She has Pete. And if necessary, Jeb can go. Gabe will have whatever he needs. Surgeons, an Air Vac, anything. My place is here with you.''

Meg saw so many things in that sculpted face, many beautiful things: friendship, loyalty, love. Jeb was wrong. This was not the face of a fallen angel, but a wounded angel.

She slid her hands free, and her palm curved around his cheek. *My place is here with you.* His words made her heart sing. ''I can get to my room alone,'' she said huskily. ''Go make your calls. Work your magic for Gabe.''

Shiloh smiled, turning his head to kiss her palm. ''I'll call when there's news.'' He stood, his fingertips stroking her hair once more, then he was gone.

Meg was alone again. A solitary figure in the waning crowd, holding his kiss in her palm. Discovering what Jeb had discovered and admitting it at last.

She loved Shiloh, the gentle warrior with the face of a wounded angel.

Six

"When Sonny turned Shadow was gone." Meg closed the book and laid it aside.

"Next time Sonny needs him Shadow will come," Eddie said.

"He's right there waiting at Sonny's heel," Tommy yawned, snuggling under the covers. "Sonny and Shadow are your best stories, Mom."

"Thank you, darling." Meg rose from the hassock she sat on and knelt over them. She kissed their soap-scented cheeks and snapped off the bedside light. "Alexis is in her room." She nodded toward the open doorway that flanked the children's room on the right as hers did on the left. "After a bath I think I'll go to bed, too. If you need me just call out."

"We'll be all right, Mom," Tommy reassured her.

"'Course," Eddie chimed in.

Meg stifled a smile as she heard the protective tone in their voices. Though they couldn't fully comprehend their circumstances, they recognized her distress and wanted to help. She adjusted the sheet then kissed them again and left the bedside. Before a crib by her door she paused. Samantha slept surrounded by a collection of plush animals. Her plump little body was sprawled in abandon. With her daughter's animated face in repose Meg saw the promise of striking beauty.

Samantha snuffled and drew her knees beneath her, curling into a ball. Meg marveled she could sleep that way, but made no attempt to move her. In the next instant the chubby little body wriggled and turned. Samantha flung her arms over her head, balanced one foot on her knee. There would be dozens of impossible contortions before the night ended.

Meg felt a rush of tenderness as she touched her fingers to her own lips then to the baby's. What changes would this wonderful creature have made in Keith's life? Could her sunny smile have won his love and kept his demons at bay? Could a daughter have done what a wife and sons could not? Sadness tainted Meg's wishful thoughts. All the dreaming in the world wouldn't change the fact that Samantha would never know her father, and the boys would forget him. He was already little more than a character in the stories she told them, and the fault was hers.

"Face sad, Ma?" Samantha's sleepy voice was like a beacon in the darkness.

"I didn't mean to wake you, darling. I'm not sad. I was thinking that you're as pretty as a flower."

"Princess. Lo Lo say me pretty princess."

Meg twined a golden curl around her finger. Letting it spring free, she wondered how Shiloh guessed what would please Samantha. He couldn't know that long before she could understand them the child had listened for hours, loving the tales of make-believe kingdoms and princesses who lived happily ever after. "He's right," she whispered softly. "You are a princess."

"Humph." The sound was a sleepy gurgle.

"I love you, princess."

"Sam love Ma, love TomEddie." Then in one drowsy sigh she added, "Love Kota, love Lo Lo. Lots."

Love was a simple thing for this uncomplicated child, Meg thought. There was either black or white, with no gray areas of doubt. She either loved or she didn't and said so. Wouldn't it be wonderful to be so open and sure? Meg touched a moist baby cheek, her fingers trailing over the rounded curve of it as she moved away. At her door she stopped. "Sweet dreams, guys. I love you."

"Too," Tommy and Eddie said in a sleepy shorthand.

"You forgot Joe," Eddie reminded.

"So I did." Meg approached the cage. The bird swayed on his perch, his feathers almost luminous. "'Night, Joe."

Joe growled, ruffled his feathers, lifted one translucent eyelid to glare at her, then hunched his head between his shoulders. Silently he settled on his perch.

"The silent type, huh?" As she moved away she heard a hint of a sound. Then heard it again.

Good night, sweetheart.

"Good night, Joe." Chuckling, she left the room.

Meg laid down her brush and looked carefully into the mirror. Her inspection had less to do with vanity than with improving her image in the eyes of her children. It hurt to know that worry for her was again creeping into their lives. What Alexis had seen in them a week ago she saw in them herself tonight, and had set about shoring up the outward signs of her composure.

After half an hour of pampering in the bath, the lines of tension had been smoothed from her face. With pumice and oil her body had been polished to a gilded elegance. Her nails were manicured; her hair had been washed and brushed to burnished ebony. Though it was still early her bed beckoned. A long sleep would complete her efforts. Tomorrow the cracks in her serenity would be less visible to her children, and they could turn their remarkable enthusiasm to the wonders of Shiloh's home.

Shiloh. How long had it been since he'd been carefree? Certainly not since she'd come into his life. Especially not in the week since Gabe's injury. After the false sighting of Ballenger the search had intensified and she had seen less of Shiloh. Suddenly he kept a distance between them, one that did not hide the gray-hued fatigue etched in his face.

Not even news that Gabe would recover had eased the drawn look for long. There was no trace of Evan Ballenger, so Shiloh drove himself harder, growing quieter and more aloof each day. When the grueling schedule claimed its reckoning, he battled alone a pain that gave no quarter.

My place is here with you. Had she dreamed those words? No. Meg shook her head slowly. She hadn't. Shiloh, who was ever loyal to his friends, had made a choice without a qualm, then had shut himself away from her.

With her hand at her cheek she stared into the mirror seeing not herself but Shiloh. Shiloh, whose wisdom gave confidence to a faltering young boy and set free his twin, who gallantly bestowed royalty on a little girl who believed in fairy tales. Shiloh, who gave, asking for nothing, accepting nothing.

Meg shivered. Fingers that ached to comfort closed around her brush, until their cramping shattered her reverie. Deliberately she laid the brush aside and folded her hands loosely in her lap. Gaze met mirrored gaze in complete concentration. She thought of love and giving and gratitude. Gratitude could be a dangerous thing. Once everything she'd felt for Shiloh had been bound up in it, blurred by it.

It was ironic that he had been on his way to the aid of a friend when she had understood the difference between gratitude and love. In that moment, as she watched him, his body strong, resolute, his dark, shaggy head inclined in thought, she knew what she felt was fiercer and less complete than gratitude. Far less complete. Complete suggested boundaries, an end. If he would accept it, her love would be boundless, unending.

"If," she whispered. Hope flickered and died before it could bloom. Heavy lids closed over dulled eyes. She sighed, her head bowed regretfully. When would she ever learn? Her romantic dreams were the dreams of a fool. He asked for nothing because he wanted nothing. Beyond his gentle compassion he was aloof. Solitary, but not lonely. This was the way he meant it to be.

He was alone, he was hurting, but he didn't need her. He didn't want her.

Meg rose, her naked body a sultry reflection against a backdrop of classic elegance. She had grown thinner, her hips leaner, her waist smaller, but her breasts were full and firm. When she slipped into her nightgown their crests were hints of rose beneath the clinging silk. As she smoothed the shimmering turquoise over her hips, lightning flickered like a blush against the sky, and thunder rumbled beyond the mountains. In quick succession the booming overture was repeated, and the querulous bass echoed over rooftops, fading into silence. A breeze gathered strength and rose to tap against her window, its low moan filling the night.

There was violence in the air, and Meg was drawn to it. Beyond her window trees swayed like ships on a frothing sea. A leaf-cloaked branch battered an angry warning against the glass. Meg stayed, mesmerized by the fury risen from the somnolent mountains, imagining she could hear over the banshee's howl the thunder of pounding hooves.

The wind threatened again and she turned to her bed, her step weary, her heart heavy for Shiloh who had only Dakota to share his pain. Her hand was at the lamp when thunder rumbled, closer, louder. A knock at her door was like a postscript.

Meg frowned and reached for her robe. Looping it loosely around her, she went to answer a second summons. She opened the door no more than a crack, then, stunned, let it swing from her nerveless fingers.

Shiloh stood in the hall, dressed for riding as she'd never seen him. His trousers were closely fitted of a fine, creamy fabric. His tailored shirt was the rich red-brown that absurdly recalled the warm scent of cinnamon to her mind. The boots he wore, unlike his usual scuffed and serviceable brown leather, were tall, black and polished to a sheen. He was leaner. The last ounce of superfluous flesh had been honed from him, leaving only bone and sinew and deeply corded muscle. His dark hair was almost too neatly brushed away from his weathered face. Soon he would run his fingers through it, mindless of the havoc they wreaked.

He was dark, brooding sensuality. He smiled at her, with that crooked half-smile that left his scar untouched, and her heart broke for the haunted sadness hidden there.

"You were expecting someone?" he asked softly.

"Of course not." She moved further into the doorway, unaware that the light behind her turned her nightclothes to a misty illusion.

Shiloh's eyes were on her. He savored in every part of himself the vision before him. Her hair was a glistening fall of darkness, her skin tawny ivory. Her body beneath the turquoise and lace was a whisper of mystery. Desire stirred, as deep as the night, as violent as the storm. It tore at him, shredding his veneer of control. She was far too beautiful, and he was tired of fighting.

"This was a mistake. I shouldn't have come." He wheeled away abruptly. "I'll send someone else."

"Shiloh! Don't!" The words tumbled from her unconsidered.

He turned, ignoring her outstretched hand. He seemed distracted, distemperate.

"Don't go." She touched him. His arm beneath the turned-back cuff of his shirt was hot and dry, but not feverish. He was not ill. As she drew him with her into the room her relief was so profound she barely remembered to question why he'd come.

He felt her hand around his wrist and knew she spoke, asked a question, made a suggestion. He had no idea which. It didn't matter. All that mattered was the pounding in his head, the throbbing of his body. One more battle of denial, when denial was the last thing he wanted. "Do you," he said. His voice was raspy. He swallowed to wet his dry throat, searching for the right mood. "Do you always dress like that to sleep alone?"

"You don't think—" Her hand went to her breasts, remembering only then that they were barely covered by the clinging lace that plunged to her waist. Her fingers clutched at the robe, gathering it over her.

"Shh, don't fret. I was only teasing." He managed a hoarse chuckle. Her astonished innocence helped. Beautiful, guileless, untouchable innocence that had more than once cooled the rage of wildfire. With her wide-eyed look of shock and hurt, he could almost make himself pretend she was a sweet, scolded child to be petted and teased into good humor. If he shut his eyes and forgot to breathe. Almost. "Don't bother twisting the life out of that robe, it's no help. In any case, it's too late."

"Too late?" Thunder rumbled, its deep roar a warning of what would come, but she barely noticed.

"I suspected you were more than lovely, Meg. The gown proves it. It matches your eyes." He took a step toward her and doubted his sanity. How could he play this role of wicked teasing when her fragrance seemed to wind around him, drawing him to her like an invisible web? He didn't mean to do it, but, damn him for a fool, he spoke his thoughts. "You smell as beautiful as you look."

Meg looked up at him, confused. His words teased but his tone was rough, forced, and his eyes danced with something more than mischief. She took a step back, giving herself space to think. "You're right," she said at last. "I don't usually dress for bed like this."

"But tonight you did."

What was it she heard in his voice and saw in his face? He had always been gentle with her, but this was more—a softness, a hesitancy. As if the armor had been stricken from him, leaving him vulnerable.

Perhaps she was imagining the whole thing! Giving herself a mental shake and drawing away from the emotional quicksand that threatened to suck her under, she chose honesty as her defense. ''Tonight I did. The children have picked up ragged vibes, so I went shopping at the boutique in the lobby. The perfume and the gown are part of a decadent indulgence.'' She whirled around, the light catching in the folds of her gown, gilding her body in blue-green fire.

''You mend ragged vibes nicely.'' Shiloh knew he had to leave before he made the mistake of his life. Before he did something that hurt her.

''I'm not so sure the edges are mended, but they've been soothed by the fuss and bother.''

Despite her claims of calm, her eyes were unnaturally bright. The strain was showing; she'd walked a tightrope of fear too long. ''You look tired,'' he said after a long pause. ''Beautiful, but tired. I can see by the bed—'' his gaze swept over the turned-back covers ''—that you were calling it a night. So I'll just take Joe and go.''

''Joe?''

''He's why I came.''

''Oh.'' She struggled against the disappointment constricting her throat.

''He hates storms. At their peak, he tries to outsing

them. Once you hear Joe sing, you'll never want to again."

"He's been quiet so far."

"These storms can rumble over the mountains for hours. He saves his voodoo, or whatever, for the worst."

"We could cover the cage."

"He'll spend days muttering that we tried to suffocate him."

"The children would hate that. What will you do with him?"

"The music room is soundproof. He can sing there to his heart's content."

"Why would he sing if he can't hear the storm?"

"He won't have to hear it. He senses when the worst has come."

"Then why not leave him here with the children?"

"Honey," Shiloh said. His grin was a little more natural. "Taking him to the music room is to protect us from Joe, not Joe from the storm."

"Surely it can't be that bad."

"So speaks an innocent." He took her chin between his forefinger and thumb. It was a spontaneous move that went dreadfully awry, and his careful pretenses betrayed him. His grin died slowly. He stroked the soft, vital fullness of her lower lip, watching her, utterly fascinated by the flash of even, white teeth beyond the tender flesh.

Around them the storm grew quiet, gathering its forces for its wildest fury. Nearby Meg's children slept. Silence became an unbroken pall between them.

Hot, lusty, male-female awareness pulsed beyond one stopping point, then another. In the far reaches of his clouded mind, Shiloh knew he should end this now. Gathering the remnants of his strength he willed himself to do what he must, to say what he should before it was too late. When he looked down into eyes that had lost their last vestige of blue and were the fathomless green of passion he learned the strength of his intent.

Principles were forfeited, promises abandoned. Joe was forgotten, and the storm. ''Meg,'' he whispered, the sound an endearment.

Meg shivered at his touch. Fire licked at the frayed edges of her false serenity, laying waste the night's mending. He was so close she could feel the heat of his body. So hot! She wondered if the same fire burned in him.

Once she had been wrong. Not this time. Not when his eyes were bluer than she'd ever seen them. Not when his riveting gaze seemed to see straight into her heart. The fire settled in the pit of her belly, its embers hotter than its flame. She trembled, yearning for his arms around her. Surely her need must be in her eyes, for his chest rose and fell in a rough breath, but he did not touch her. Only his thumb stroked her lips. Gently. Maddeningly.

She didn't think it or plan it, but a part of her wanted more of him. Of its own volition her tongue touched the tip of his thumb, tasting the salty, smoky taste, electrifying her.

Shiloh groaned. His hand slid into the heavy fall

of her hair. He took the final step, fitting the hard planes of his body to the rounded, welcoming curves of hers. ''Meg.'' His lips were against her hair, his breath stirring an errant strand. ''Sweet, sweet Meg.''

Beloved, her heart answered. She dared not say a word. Not yet. Not until she was sure he wanted it. For now she would content herself with the touch of his lips against her temple, the pounding rush of his heart against hers. There would be time later to understand the moment.

Without warning the lamp flickered and died. In the cavernous darkness the storm woke, howling its wrath, lighting the sky with its incandescence, turning night to fleeting day. As suddenly as it had come the brilliance faded, leaving the room in Cimmerian blackness.

With blinded eyes, Meg found her world in Shiloh. His lips were like warm honey, his arms her comfort. The clean, unadorned scent of him sent arrows of pleasure coursing through her.

''Shiloh.'' The thread of her thought was lost when he moved languorously against her, leaving no doubt of the state of his needs. ''Please,'' she began but never finished her plea.

The storm chose that moment to quieten as suddenly as it had risen. The lamp flickered and grew steadily brighter. Somewhere in the depths of the inn a motor hummed as its systems sprang to life. Eddie cried out in his sleep. Samantha's crib creaked as she shifted and turned. A low, querulous voice muttered in some rough, unintelligible language.

"Uh-oh. Joe." Shiloh laughed wryly, shakily.

"A serenade?"

"I'm afraid so." He linked his fingers at the nape of her neck, leaning his forehead to hers. "I should take him and go."

"Will it be that bad?"

"Worse."

A grumble from the next room served as an urgent reminder that time was short.

"I do have to leave." Shiloh lifted his head, his hands moving to her shoulders, reluctant to let her go.

"I know." Her eyes were on him, hungry for him.

"Would you—"

"What?" Meg waited.

"Nothing," Shiloh's voice was hoarse with finality. His hands fell to his side, his fingers curling emptily. He couldn't ask her to come with him. If she did he would take her to his bed, consequences and promises be damned, and perhaps himself as well.

"A pretty disturbing nothing, I'd say." Impulsively she stroked the scar that twisted fiercely with his scowl.

"It was a foolish notion." He moved from her touch, his frown fading, a bland expression coming down over his face like a curtain. "I'll take Joe now."

"Of course." Meg bowed her head, hiding the lost, baffled look she knew was in her eyes. She folded her fingers in her palm, keeping the warmth of his cheek with her for a precious moment.

Leading him to the children's room, she waited silently as he stood near their beds. His gaze fondly touched each child, the small hurtful half-smile on his lips.

"Your children are beautiful." Before she could reply he lifted the cage from its hook and, with no goodbye, he left her.

Meg paced the length of her room. Once she caught sight of herself, a forlorn little figure in a ridiculously grand gown. She marched to the dresser intending to change into a pale yellow gown that was comfortable if not exciting. Then, remembering that Shiloh had called her lovely, she stopped.

Lovely! Yet in the midst of the excitement that passed like a current between them he had withdrawn. Easily, unconcerned, as he always had. "No! This time was different. Shiloh was different."

There had been something new in the way he looked at her, in his touch. She'd heard something bittersweet and poignant in the sound of her name on his lips. Tonight had been a turning point but she hadn't understood why.

"What is it that I don't see?" Meg sank onto the edge of her bed, her hands clasped tightly in her lap. Her sightless gaze moved to some nonexistent dimension, seeking an equally nonexistent guidance. "What should I understand?"

Her mind sifted through the little she knew of Shiloh. Some items were factual, some were supposition, some were admittedly fantasy. Were they part of her answer?

"The face of a demon, the courage of a lion, the

heart of a wounded angel,'' she whispered. Bitterness, conviction, compassion, The integral parts that were Shiloh.

Once she'd wondered why there was no woman with whom he could build a life, nor had there ever been. Why? Meg had asked herself endlessly. Any woman would want Shiloh.

Was there never a woman who could teach him what he feels and make him face it? Could that be it? Did he not understand or believe his own feelings? Was she the woman who could teach him? Had she the strength? It wouldn't be sweetness and light, but for the woman who dared and won, it would be wonderful.

To live in the civilized world after ten years of brutality would be difficult. Those who succeeded had done it with consummate gentleness and fierce dedication. Shiloh was one of that wild, rare breed. To match such fierceness with her love, to tame it, would make her the richest of women.

''I'd never want to tame Shiloh. Never!'' she burst out. But wouldn't the word serve to describe the concessions such a man would make if he cared? He would always be wild, he would always be free, but he would temper them with love.

''He *does* care. I've seen it in his look, felt it in his touch. Why does he back away?'' Had the ugliness of his life made him think he was incapable of loving? ''No! No!'' Meg cried, her fist drumming at her knee in rhythm with her protest. ''He has more love to give than anyone I've ever known.''

...one who would teach him what he feels and make him face it. Her own words. He was different tonight, at least for a little while. Open, approachable, as if he was reaching out to her. *Could* she teach him? *Could* she show him how very much love he had to give?

"What if I'm wrong?" Her voice sank to a ragged whisper. "Dear God! What if I'm wrong? I have been before."

She clasped her hands over her mouth, wishing for someone to turn to. Jeb, who knew Shiloh as few did, or Caroline with her incomparable sense of truth. Meg shivered. There was no Jeb, no Caroline; there were only Shiloh and herself, and the specter of Ballenger who had brought them together.

Unconsciously she rose to pace again. Her gown swirled around her as she turned and paced and turned again. Her arms were crossed at her breasts, her hands kneading the taut muscles of her shoulders. Her eyes ached with the effort of her thoughts. Snapping off the lamp by the bedside offered no relief. Darkness brought with it memories of Shiloh. The feel of him, his small, vulnerable smile, his masculine scent.

From out of the night the storm seemed to beckon her. Meg whirled, racing to the window. Lightning streaked over the meadow, an eerie iridescence that died in a crash of thunder. But not before she saw the dark, melded forms of man and horse racing like the wind.

The sheer curtain fluttered in her face. She grasped it, holding it aside with a white-knuckled fist. He shouldn't ride. The storm was too close. Yet she knew he had to. It was his weapon against pain that could turn his scarred eye to a burning coal of ice blue and his face to ash beneath the darkening brand.

He had no one to turn to, either. Only Dakota.

She understood now the softness in him, the unguardedness. He had waged his own quiet battle with torment, and that strong front he always presented wavered but hadn't crumbled. He might even have been tempted to seek solace from another human being. But that moment was fleeting. Now he rode like a centaur.

Meg's eyes never left the powerful figures challenging the storm. Long after horse and rider had disappeared from view she watched, wondering what would become of them, of Shiloh and herself. She pressed her fingers against the cool windowpane, daring to dream. "Be safe, my love," she whispered and turned away to her bed.

Meg tossed then turned. The cool room should have been pleasant but the air was oppressive. With each restless move her hair wound around her, clinging like a sticky mist, and her tangled gown imprisoned her legs. The tick of the clock grew louder than the storm. Each second dragged by until Meg found herself holding her breath wondering if the sound of its passing would ever come. Sleep was hopeless. The peace she courted had flown in the wind with the pounding of Dakota's hooves. She lay, eyes wide in the darkness, throat dry, waiting.

At first she thought the clock had gone mad, ranting

at the night like an insane magpie. Then she knew. The wild, frenzied drumming was the sound she had waited for. Throwing aside the rumpled sheet she dashed to the window. There, on the ridge, with the wind swirling around him and a flickering radiance limning him against the horizon, was Shiloh.

Long after the glare had died he was drawn in fire and darkness in her mind. He was weary and hurting and had no one to comfort him. It was written in every proud line of his body.

"I can," Meg whispered to the wind, to the storm.

As she watched, transfixed, the heavens opened, sending rain like streamers of tinsel over the hillside, and Shiloh was running before it. His body matched the powerful rhythm of the horse as they rose in wild abandon over shrub and fence. Suddenly his head was thrown back; his shoulders heaved. For Meg the low, aching moan of the wind became his lonely cry.

"My poor Shiloh." Unshed tears trembled in his name, and her heart was breaking for this proud, lonely man.

Turning from the window she snatched her robe from the back of a chair. Tying it securely she hurried to the children. Touching and tucking, she assured herself that all was well. In the room beyond, Alexis's lamp was out. But the night-light the governess kept burning marked her way to them in case of emergency.

All this, the safety, the security was because of Shiloh—who asked nothing for himself. He would not ask; Meg understood that now, but she could offer.

Fear of rejection and its pain were almost palpable, yet this was a gamble worth taking. He must know that someone cared that he hurt and brought comfort, not pity.

If he faced what he felt, perhaps he would discover that he did care, that his place truly was with her.

The rain was nearer; scattered drops were falling faster. He would be wet. From the bath she took two huge towels. Draping them over her arm, she sped from the room, pausing only long enough to engage the lock. Her bare feet hardly touched the floor. At the service stair her gown trailed over worn treads. Once through the secluded door she had only to follow the path that led to the barn and Shiloh.

Seven

He was there. A single electric lantern lit the stall where he worked, readying Dakota for the night.

Meg stepped farther into the old barn. A covering of clean straw muffled her footsteps, catching at the hem of her gown as she moved past rough-hewn stone walls and massive beams silvered by age. The barn was a landmark, a magical blending of dusty southern antiquity and simple lines. But she was conscious only of Shiloh—his hair tousled, glistening with raindrops like beads of jet; his face flushed, euphoric in defiance of the storm; his wet shirt clinging as he stroked the horse with a loving hand.

Meg paused beyond the circle of light. With the towels almost forgotten she waited.

''Whoa, fella,'' Shiloh said as the horse pranced

away, tossing its head, eyes rolling at Meg. ''Easy now, you've had more than enough for tonight, settle down.''

''Perhaps I disturbed him.'' Meg was surprised and pleased that her voice was steady when the sight of him had sent her pulse into a bruising, breath-stealing throb.

Shiloh wheeled around with the quickness of a cat. ''What are you doing out in this rain?''

''It isn't raining heavily. Not here. Not yet. You won the race.''

He stared at her, his gaze wandering over her. Slowly he folded his arms over his chest. The lines of his face were grim, his expression unreadable. ''How do you know that?''

''You were on the hillside, daring the storm to beat you. Then you were running before the wind, with the rain at your heels.''

Nothing about Shiloh changed, not the blue, blazing gaze, not the implacable grimness. Meg wondered if this was anger. Anger that she'd seen him. Did he think she spied? ''I couldn't sleep after all so I went to the window to watch the storm.'' She offered the explanation lamely. When he didn't speak she held the towels out to him. ''I thought you might need these.''

''You shouldn't be here.'' He ignored the towels. The anger in his face was readable now. ''Where was security? Why were you allowed to wander alone in the darkness?''

''I'm sure I was never truly alone, Shiloh. Someone

was certainly nearby. No one stopped me because no one ever has. Our guards have never presumed to be our keepers. You granted us freedom of the grounds; they've respected that freedom." She almost sagged in relief. He was not angry, at least not at her. Boldly, wryly, she commented, "Considering my dress, or lack of it, do you think anyone in his right mind would ask where I was going, and why?"

"Dammit, Meg. You have no business here in the barn, in this weather."

"A little rain can't hurt me, and you set the boundaries," she reminded him mildly.

"I should have excluded the barn."

"But you didn't." She stepped closer, her hands still outstretched, their uncertain trembling hidden by the folds of the towels. "Some of the rain caught you. Your shirt's wet. You could at least take as good care of yourself as you do your horse and use these to dry with. Or," she said with a touch of mischief, "would you rather have a horse blanket?"

The first glimmerings of a begrudging smile cracked the frozen mask of Shiloh's face. His lips didn't exactly lift in an engaging grin, but the stark lines eased as he stepped from Dakota's stall and latched the door.

"These would be smoother, and they certainly smell a lot better," Meg insisted when he still did not take the towels.

Shiloh chuckled. "Little witch," he murmured, his gaze still holding hers. Slowly, not looking away, he began to open his shirt. As the last button slipped free, he slid the clammy fabric from his shoulders and hung the shirt on a hook. His fingers brushed hers as he took a single towel. His expression changed. His grin became a grimace in the instant before his face was buried in the deep terry.

Meg had never seen him undressed. Clothed, his lean, hard body had been vigor and strength and unconscious elegance, but nothing in her life had prepared her for the rough splendor of a half-naked Shiloh. She watched as deeply corded muscles that had strained beneath the clinging fabric of his shirt flexed and rippled seductively beneath the taut, bronzed skin. Not even the hideous scars of war that marked his back and shoulders could distort the hypnotic motion.

Her throat ached with the rush of unshed tears as she realized he had grown thinner in the weeks she'd known him. His dedication to the Sullivans, and the pain it wrought, had taken its pound of flesh several times over. If Shiloh would demand this much of himself for her sake, for the children, surely it meant they were more than a passing interest, more than the Samaritan's good deed or Galahad's damsel in distress.

"You shouldn't look at me like that."

Shiloh's hoarse voice broke into her thoughts. He had grown still beneath her stare, the towel against the curve of his neck, his hand motionless.

"I like to look at you," she said simply, because there could be nothing but honesty between them now.

"I know." His hand closed so tightly over the

towel she thought it would tear. "I've tried not to see it, but it's been there, in your eyes. Can you imagine what I feel when I see that softness in you?"

Meg looked away, unable to hold his fierce gaze, wanting to hear, but afraid. This was the time predestined on that hot, sultry day he had waited in the shadowy cool of her home. He waited now. The path they took would be her choice.

With her eyes closed, her hands clasped before her, she wondered if her decision had been as preordained as this moment. She lifted her head, her gaze meeting his, holding it, the only sound the wild keening of the wind. "Here," she murmured softly, moving closer, taking the towel from his hand. "Let me do that."

"Meg." Her name was a low, strangled sound.

"Hush," she scolded, touching his lips with the tip of her fingers, caressing them. "For once in your life let someone do something for you."

"Witch," he said again. "Sometimes I think you were created to torment me." His voice was rough and grating but he stood placidly beneath the stroke of her hands.

There was love in her fingers as she dried him with the care she once lavished on her babies. She swallowed hard and forced herself not to gasp as she saw how terrible his wounds had been. Jeb was right; he had been hurt in so many ways. What wounds lay beneath the surface? How awful were they?

Meg dropped the damp towel in the hay and slowly stepped away, her eyes moving from his body to his face. With her bare hand she brushed away the rain that clung to the scarred brow and cheek. His jaw tightened but he didn't draw away. Encouraged, she grew more confident, her fingers massaging the clenched muscles at his temple.

''Meg.'' There was a hint of warning in his tone, but no anger. ''Don't.'' He frowned, and a sheen of sweat beaded his forehead, but he could make no move to stop her.

''I know, I know.'' She crooned tender absurdities that soothed, persuaded. Slowly she felt the knotted muscles begin to relax. ''I know you think I shouldn't, but you give no reason. You've been so kind and caring, how could it be wrong to return a part of that caring?''

''Because—'' He bit the word off, stumbling over it. He closed his eyes almost fiercely, needing to lock himself from the sight of her to say what he must.

Suddenly Meg was afraid. She wanted to run, to seek refuge in the storm, letting its light blind, its furor deafen. Then she need not face the hurt that might come. But she couldn't. Once, a lifetime ago, she'd run from failure and the end had been disastrous. This time she knew the risks. Shiloh might reject the little she could offer him: herself, her love. She had gambled, all her cards were played. The last card was his. She wouldn't run away this time.

Her hand had ceased its tender ministration, her fingers rested against his throbbing temple. ''Tell me, Shiloh,'' she whispered. ''Please.''

He still did not look at her. His lashes were an ebony smudge beneath his eyes. A ragged sound rose from deep in his chest, and his breath was uneven. "You mustn't," he said at last. "Because when you look at me or touch me, like a fool I think you want me as badly as I want you."

For Meg, it seemed as if the sun chose a single spot to grace with life-giving warmth in the midst of the storm. If he hadn't said all she needed to hear, it didn't matter. He wanted her. It was a beginning. Oh, yes! It was just the beginning. Deliberately she moved her hand from his face, letting it drift over his shoulder to his chest, lingering at the flat, male nipple, teasing lightly downward to his low-riding belt, then moving completely away from his tense body. Lost without the feel of his skin beneath her hands she said simply, "I do want you, very badly."

"You've confused gratitude for something more," he said in a strange stilted tone.

"I haven't."

"I'm nearly forty. You're barely thirty with so much of your life ahead of you. You can't want an old battle-scarred warrior like me."

She knew his eyes were on her, burning with an intensity that she thought could pierce her soul. Flowery phrases and grandiose persuasions had no part of what was between them. The words were unadorned, but they came straight from her heart when she said again, "I want you."

She heard his breath rasp in his struggle for control. Then as if he must see for himself his hands burrowed beneath her hair, cupping the back of her head, lifting her face to his. Meg expected a nervous blush to rise, turning her cheeks a telltale pink, but she found herself perfectly composed. She could meet his searching gaze serenely. "I love you, Shiloh," she said in a low voice. "I have for a long time."

Shiloh did not speak, but something flared in his eyes. Before she could interpret it his head was descending toward hers; his lips were touching hers. Once like a summer breeze, then again, tantalizing, promising the dark, sweet mysteries of himself. When he moved away with a regretful growl, Meg rose on tiptoe, her face lifted, her mouth offering more, wanting more.

"Sweetheart, don't." Despite his cry, and before he could stop himself, his hands closed over her shoulders, holding her, sliding down her back to her hips, drawing her nearer until the fullness of her silk-clad breasts teased his naked chest. Her hair brushed his chin, surrounding him in the aura of her fragrance. The touch of her lips at his throat became the torch to waiting tinder. His warning was forgotten.

The power of desire was greater than his own strength, and his thirst for her ruled his head as well as his body. Meg deserved more than the impermanence he represented, but not even his conscience could stop him now. Perhaps it never would have stopped him. When she stepped from the shadows with her turquoise nightclothes turned to clinging blue fire by the light of the lantern, he knew he must have her. His protests had been a charade, doomed from the start. The time for proud delusions had ended. He swung her into his arms and mounted the little-used stairs that led to the loft.

The hay was newly dried, the scent of it the heady perfume of endless summer days and lazy loving. Meg burrowed her head into Shiloh's shoulder, her lips hungering to touch again the hot flesh of his throat. This was wanting, needing, as she'd never known it. When he set her on her feet and moved to turn on the light of a weak, naked bulb she murmured a plaintive protest.

"I want to see you. I won't hurt you. I promised I never would." He felt a flicker of guilt and hoped his promise wasn't empty, but not even guilt could cool the flames that consumed him. Only Meg could quench them with her passion. He would remember for both that her spirit was far stronger than her delicate body. He must remember for himself what a fragile treasure she was. "Don't be afraid, Meg. Not of me."

There was so much she wanted to tell him. That it wasn't the light, that she needed him, that she would never be afraid of anything as long as he held her. She wanted to tell him but the forgotten towel was spread over the hay. Her robe was drawn down her arms and tossed aside. Then Shiloh was sliding the straps of her gown from her shoulders, letting the silk float down her body to gather like a mist at her feet.

An unsteady hand caressed her cheek, her throat, her breasts, bringing to their crests the dark, rich hue of a rose. "Do you have any idea how beautiful you are?"

"No." She meant to say she was not beautiful, but his hand explored further and there was no thought for more.

"You are God's most perfect creation. So lovely here, and here." His lips began to trace the path his hand had followed and Meg doubted that her legs would support her.

"I'm not beautiful," she denied in a voice she did not recognize as her own.

"You are. You are. There's never been anyone like you." He took her hand and drew her down with him. The towel was velvet beneath her skin, the hay a cushion. The long legs entwining with hers were strong and warm. She wondered when he had removed the rest of his clothing, but he touched her again and she found she no longer cared.

Shiloh ached for her as he hadn't known he could. How long had he dreamed that she would someday be lying beside him, her lovely body his for the taking, her eyes bright with desire? How long had he wanted to bury himself in her, joining their bodies, making her his? How long!

"A lifetime," he muttered and could wait no longer. He covered her body with his, her breasts cushioning him, her thighs parting to receive him. Her body yielded, then moved with his, accepting the languid, caressing strokes. Her head tossed, her hair swept over the hay, a river of darkness against the gold. A sheen of moisture painted her body with silvered drops. She murmured something he didn't understand. Her hands were at his back, her nails digging into his flesh. She arched urgently against him in a driving rhythm, taking him deeper into herself.

His ravenous hunger was unleashed, the wish to be gentle forgotten. Answering her fierce demand he sought to ease his sweet torment in her pulsing depths. A desperate cry. A ragged sound torn from his throat as the searing heat of their passion exploded like flames in the darkness. She was his! She had given herself to him and would never belong to another. A savage pleasure gripped him in this total possession. Something he'd never wanted or needed before. When one loved, the simple physical act became more—more than pleasure, more than procreation. It was the bonding of heart and soul and mind.

When one loved. Words he'd never thought, never said. Not to any woman. Words that transformed him. As he plunged harder and deeper, sheathing himself again and again within her, her sweet cry quelled the savage hunger that drove him, filling him with a tenderness that left him shaken. A tenderness that created its own exquisite pleasure sent him crashing with her into the ecstasy of fulfillment.

Meg cried out once more, embracing him, her shuddering body slowly subsiding, nestling beneath his. Shiloh leaned over her, discovering she was even more beautiful with her mouth swollen from his kisses and her hair tumbling over one breast. Clothing became her, but with her body moist and glowing from the exertions of their lovemaking she was magnificent.

He wanted to tell her she had brought beauty and

joy into his life. His voice dropped to a dulcet whisper. His words were that wicked, intoxicating nonsense only lovers say.

Meg clung to him, listening as a child does to a wonderful fairy tale. Not truly believing, but wishing she could. The smile she gave him was heartbreakingly lovely. A tear clung to a dark lash then fell like a glittering crystal on her flushed cheek.

He leaned closer, capturing the tear with his tongue, savoring the salty, sweet taste of her. This was part of Meg, and she was his.

Thunder rocked the barn on its foundation, and rain pounded the tin roof in a sudden roar. Meg's body quickened, startled from the languid aftermath of their love. "Shh," he comforted, gathering her closer into his arms. "It's just the rain. It won't last long. The worst is nearly over. Listen. You can hear each drop dancing over the roof."

"Not dancing," Meg said, soothed by his tranquil voice. "They're singing. A lullaby, I think."

"A special lullaby for you." He leaned over her, content now to simply hold her. "I promised I'd watch over you as you slept. Sleep now. I'll be here."

Meg smoothed a lock of hair from his face, her fingers finding the scar, remembering his pain. "My beautiful Shiloh."

He chuckled softly. "You must be crazy. No one's ever called this mug beautiful."

"Beautiful," she said stubbornly as she drifted further into sleep. "Hurt. Sorry."

He chuckled again at her childlike frown. "Don't

be. I don't hurt anymore.'' It was true. He didn't hurt. That bitter disappointment that seethed within him like a festering wound had been exorcised. Nothing had really changed; it couldn't. But somehow when he held this gentle, passionate woman in his arms, it no longer mattered. Nothing mattered but Meg, and that he keep her safe. ''Sleep, love,'' he murmured. ''Sleep and let me hold you.''

''Love,'' Meg murmured and snuggled farther into the arms that would be her shelter from the world.

Bare-chested and barefoot, Shiloh stood before the window. One hand was braced against the massive frame, the other plunged deeply in the pocket of his slacks. The storm had passed, leaving its mark. But he saw none of it through panes darkened by a starless night. He saw only the reflection of Meg, sleeping peacefully in his bed. Her body was hardly a ripple beneath the pale blue sheet. Her hair tumbled over a bare shoulder; heavy lashes clung like a veil to her cheeks. He had sat by her side for hours, remembering.

She had been wonderful. The look in her eyes when she touched him had not been pity. It had been pain, *his* pain, taken as her own. He had let her into the sanctum of his heart. Why Meg? What was different about this woman? Why had her memory haunted him for so long? How had she swept away his armor and made him glad she did?

Meg sighed, and Shiloh smiled at the sound. He turned from the reflection, hungering for the loveliness of reality. With his body aching he moved silently to her. He wanted to kiss her awake and lie with her on the crisp sheets of his bed. His bed. His woman. How would he live without her now that he'd found her?

Meg stirred again, her mouth turned up in a smile. "Shiloh?" Her voice was blurred with sleep.

"I'm here."

She half rose, bracing herself on one elbow, trying to clear the cobwebs of sleep from her mind. "Where are we?"

"This is my suite."

"The barn!"

"It happened. It wasn't a dream." He sat on the edge the bed, taking her hand in his. "We made love with straw as our bed, then you slept. When the storm ended I brought you here because I couldn't bear to let you go. Not yet."

"You should have awakened me."

"I wanted you to rest."

"Did you sleep?"

"Not this time."

"It's nearly dawn! You must be exhausted." She bolted upright, realizing too late the sheet was her only covering.

Her nakedness seemed to disturb her. Shiloh lifted her palm to his lips. Then, releasing her, he rose to stride to a closet. From it he took a white cotton shirt. "Wear this," he said as he drew it around her shoulders and helped her slide her arms into the sleeves. He folded back the cuffs, then buttoned each button until the last beautiful inch of her was hidden. Running his fingers under her hair he pulled it free of the collar, letting it drift down her back. "I like to look at you," he said hoarsely. "But I know you're not accustomed to a man's eyes on your body."

"Thank you." Her eyes were huge and bright, and only the gratitude in them kept him from slipping the shirt from her shoulders and taking her in his arms.

"I think Samantha will look very much like you when she's older. She'll be beautiful as your child would be." Meg's face changed. Suddenly the brightness dimmed; her eyes were troubled.

"Meg? You look frightened. What's wrong?" She looked away. Shiloh grasped her shoulders. "Are you ill?"

"No," she managed. "I'm stupid, not ill."

"Then tell me what's wrong."

"Yes. I have to tell you. Then you might hate me."

"Honey, nothing could make me hate you."

"Not even if I'm pregnant?"

"What?" Shiloh was stunned. He released her and stood, looking at his empty hands as if they perplexed him.

Meg threw back the covers, pacing to the window. Her back was turned, her body shaking. "With my track record it's more than possible."

"Meg, you're not making sense."

She faced him. "I haven't practiced birth control since Keith died. There was no reason. Tonight I didn't think."

''You're afraid you might have conceived my child!''

''I'm sorry, Shiloh,'' she said raggedly and seemed even smaller in his shirt. ''So sorry.''

He went to her, drawing her into his arms, holding her shivering body against his. Rocking her in his embrace, he let her emotional outburst run its course. There were no tears, only hard, convulsive shudders that seemed to tear at her. Long after the last sob had subsided he stroked her, soothing her, until she was composed enough to hear him. At last he released her and stepped away. Then, framing her face with his hands, he spoke softly, wistfully. ''I wish you could have my child. There's nothing I would want more than to see my son or my daughter growing inside you, but, it isn't possible.''

''Not…not possible?'' Her eyes were wide, questioning, searching his.

''No,'' he said quietly. ''It isn't possible. But if it were, the responsibility for tonight wouldn't be just yours.''

''What are you saying?''

''That you have nothing to fear.''

''Shiloh, what are you really saying?''

''I'm telling you I'm sterile.''

''Sterile?'' she said as if its meaning escaped her.

''The counterpart of my more visible war wounds.'' There was no bitterness in him. Once he hadn't accepted his fate with as much grace. Until Meg.

Images flashed through Meg's mind. Shiloh and her

children, laughing, playing. His reverent gentleness with Samantha. Shiloh who loved all children passionately, whose visible scars were the least of his wounds. Who would never have a child of his own.

"Don't cry." He wiped a tear from her cheek. "It happened a long time ago, on the other side of the world. All the tears of a lifetime won't change it." This time when he held her it was he who found comfort. Her arms around him were solace for lost dreams. He felt her unspoken grief, and grief shared is the lesser. "Now you know the secrets of Shiloh Butler. What makes him run. What he runs from."

There was a touch of wry humor in him, but Meg heard the familiar note of sadness. "What makes Shiloh run?" she said into his shoulder. "I think nothing on earth."

"Honey, I've been running for years."

Not out of fear for yourself, Meg thought, but to keep from inflicting your sorrow and bitterness on others. "We all have, for one reason or another."

Shiloh locked his hands at her waist. Her tears had stopped, but evidence of them still lingered on her lashes. She had never been more lovely. "What makes you run, Meg?"

"Many things." Her voice was a rusty sound. "Bats, spiders, myself. The foolish things I do."

"There are worse things then running."

"What could be worse than not facing our problems?"

"Dwelling on them, giving them more importance

than they deserve. Not accepting the things we can't change.''

''Can you accept what you can't change?''

''Yes, now. Can you?''

''I don't know what you mean.''

''Don't you?'' He took her right hand in his, his thumb turning the plain gold band. ''Then why this, Meg? If you still loved Keith it would be on your left hand. Do you wear it as a reminder? Are you punishing yourself for something?''

She pulled her hand from his grasp, turning from him. Leaning her forehead against the window, she felt the cool panes against her heated skin. He had a right to know of her cowardice. ''Keith and I had a good marriage in the beginning,'' she began. ''We were classic proof that opposites attract. He was older. He was a loner, abandoned, raised in foster homes. I had my parents until a boating accident when I was sixteen. Then there was my Great-Aunt Dolly. I was twenty-one when she died. Until then I had never been alone in my life. That's when I met Keith.

''I was an only child and he had no family at all, so we decided we would create our own. He was proud of the twins at first.'' She shivered and scrubbed at her cold arms with her hands. ''Then he began to change. Little things happened that I tried to ignore. By the time I admitted we were in serious trouble, I was expecting Samantha. I hoped news of the baby would change Keith back to the man I married.''

"Instead matters got worse?"

"Much worse. He began to drink heavily. Sometimes all night and into the next day."

"And eventually the next and the next after that."

"No." Meg stared down at the carpet. "That came after I told him I was leaving."

"Let me finish for you." There was a hard edge of anger in his tone. "Instead of getting the help he needed to keep you, he drank more. When he ran out of booze he got in the car, over your protest." He waited for her nod of confirmation before he continued. "He went looking for more liquor. Instead he smashed into the Ballengers' car and left them to die."

Meg was shivering uncontrollably. He wanted to hold her and make her forget the tragedies. First he had to understand what part of this horror she considered hers. "It was *Keith* who destroyed himself, not you."

She was silent for a long time, then guilt came tumbling from her. "If I hadn't said I was leaving he wouldn't have gotten so much worse. If I'd tried harder instead of planning to run away the Ballengers might be alive. And Keith might be, too. My children might have a father."

"Meg, what have you done to yourself?" He slid his arms around her, drawing her against him. "What happened to Keith and the Ballengers was never your fault."

"You don't understand."

"Some things are beyond our control. You tried.

Keith wouldn't listen. Your only hope for yourself and your children was to leave."

"No!"

"You forget I knew Keith. I knew that when he drank he could be ugly." He felt the sudden quickening of her body and knew he was right. "He'd hit you."

"He never hurt the children."

"He would've, if you'd stayed."

"I can't be sure."

"You couldn't take the chance." Though she denied his logic he had sensed a subtle easing of her tension. Her body was no longer stiff and cold. Her hands did not grip her arms so cruelly. "You made the decision you had to make. The day you believe that, you'll take off that ring.

"Look," he continued quietly, tightening his embrace. Beyond the window a fine line of molten red had begun to rim the mountaintops. "Sunrise."

"Another day."

"Yes."

"I should go. I want to be there when the children wake."

"I'll walk you across the hall." There was a quiet, imperative rap at the door. "We seem to have company. Insistent company," he added as the rapping grew louder.

"Shiloh!" The door swung open, and Jeb stepped in. "Trouble. Samantha's gone."

"What?" Shiloh reached instinctively for Meg.

"Alexis checked on them. Meg's door was ajar and

Samantha was gone.'' Softening the blow he added, ''She can't be far; her bed was still warm.''

''Samantha?'' Meg said numbly. The world was spinning beneath her, but panic would not serve her child. Taking a deep calming breath she asked, ''What do we do?''

Shiloh saw her effort and the toll it took. ''This might be nothing. She might simply have wandered away.''

''How? Where?''

Her answer was a shrill, challenging trumpeting from the barn, followed by Alexis's command, ''No, Dakota! Down!''

Eight

They ran, Jeb leading and Shiloh at Meg's side. More than once her feet left the floor, his arm her steady support. She had no memory of descending the stairs, only of suddenly bursting into the dawn.

The rambling path to the barn was too long. At Shiloh's direction they sprinted through a copse of low shrubs and scaly-barked trees. Thorny brush whipped her bare legs. A tree limb clawed at her billowing shirt, nearly ripping it from her shoulders. She hardly noticed. Chilled to the marrow with fear for Samantha, neither pain nor Shiloh's hand over hers could reach her.

The barn, once a misty, romantic place, was blasted by the white glare of floodlights. As their mad race ended in a pool of brightness Meg flinched, the beams striking her like a laser. Her impulse was to run into the barn, but something in Shiloh's face forbade it. She stood, trembling, half afraid she would find Samantha beyond that cavernous passage, half-afraid she wouldn't.

Shiloh's instinct said Samantha was here. In his gut reaction to Jeb's interruption of the foolish interlude with Meg, Ballenger was never a factor. Hunches had saved him time and again. This wasn't the occasion to question an inherent wisdom. Doubts of his intelligence could come later.

"Cass," Shiloh barked at a man nearby. "Explain."

"The little one's in a stall with Dakota. Alexis is with them. I thought it best to wait for you. Dakota's not friendly to crowds. From the sound of him more excitement might be too much." As Cass delivered his report, Meg recognized him as the stable master, whom she'd seen but never met.

"Thank God you heard the commotion from your cottage and had sense enough to know rushing in would only make things worse. Why didn't you stop Alexis?"

"She discovered the little tyke, stayed because she thought the child might be frightened." Cass was speaking very rapidly.

Meg moved fretfully, confused by the delay. The stallion screamed again, and panic clotted her throat. Samantha, her exuberant loving child, who one day would grow up to be a beautiful princess, could be crushed beneath those pounding hooves. She couldn't wait.

"No!" Shiloh read her intention, catching at her sleeve. "Stay with Jeb."

"I can't!" Frantically she tried to free herself.

Nothing could dissuade her, and he hadn't the time to try. "Come with me then, but keep out of sight." Dakota trumpeted, the cry shredding the air. Shiloh had never heard the horse in such a frenzy. Clasping Meg's hand in his, he stepped into the barn.

The scene was straight from a nightmare. Alexis stood in the stall, clad in her nightclothes. Her lips moved, their sound lost in the thud of flying hooves. Crouched in a corner clutching a tattered teddy bear was Samantha. The little girl watched as the horse pounded the floor.

"Alexis," Shiloh said softly, moving behind her, stopping beyond the stall. "Do as I say, carefully." She didn't respond. By the slight shift of her shoulders he knew she heard. One small success when the smallest detail counted. He spoke in a resonant monotone, keeping the strain from his voice. "Don't make any sudden moves. Back out slowly."

Alexis took a step back, then—toe-to-heel—another. She moved cautiously, her eyes riveted on horse and child. If she tripped, God alone could know what would happen. Slowly, inch by agonizing inch, she backed to the open gate and stepped through it. Collapsing against a stone wall she whispered, "He wouldn't let me near her."

Shiloh touched her shoulder, his eyes communicating his dread. His voice was a low rumble meant only for Alexis. "Take care of Meg. Whatever happens."

"Of course."

His fingers tightened in gratitude, then from a rack on a wall beyond, he took a rifle, loaded it with consummate skill and entered the stall. "Easy, boy, easy," he chanted. The stallion did not react. His black flanks were lathered from his thrashing, his breath labored and fetid with fear. His eyes were rolled back until they were more white than dark.

Shiloh had little hope of stopping the hooves that flashed nearer and nearer the child. He spoke once more in a low singsong croon that met with no success. He couldn't delay. He set the rifle against his shoulder. His vision blurred; his hands shook. Only desperation forced him to stand fast. His finger, when he rested it on the trigger, was steady. Dakota's head was in his sight.

With a sudden lunge, his mane flying, Dakota ducked his massive head, biting at the ground, then flinging back again to send something sailing from the stall. Refusing to be distracted, standing with his legs braced apart, aware that one shot was all he had, Shiloh resighted. His target: the wild heart.

Samantha mustn't be in the line of fire. His shot must be timed so Dakota's fall wouldn't crush her. Sweat trickled into his burning eyes as he waited for his one perfect chance. His finger began again the slow, easy pressure he needed to destroy Dakota.

"Shiloh! No!" Alexis's voice cracked like the rifle.

There was more, but Shiloh didn't hear. Incredibly Dakota stopped his rampage, his head lowered to snuffle gently at the child. Samantha's peal of laughter was as shocking as the abrupt hush that roared in his ears. The child who should have been petrified giggled and petted Dakota as if he were a kitten.

"Princess," Shiloh began a warning but Samantha cut him short.

"Nake, Lo Lo. Kota kilt a nake." Struggling to her baby legs, she toddled fearlessly past those sharp hooves.

Shiloh snatched her into his arms, feeling the mad pounding of his heart against her fragile body. "A snake?"

"Yep," Samantha said with aplomb.

"Princess." Shiloh lifted her chin, looking into her face. "Think carefully, this is very, very important. Did the snake hurt you?"

"Nope. Kota kilt him. Kilt him dead!"

Shiloh looked at Dakota. The one thing the horse hated more than the confining stall was a snake. Shiloh had seen one other encounter. Dakota had pounded the poor creature for a quarter hour before he was convinced it was properly killed.

Tonight he had suffered a stall and a snake and acquitted himself well.

"Far better than I," Shiloh muttered. In the throes of lust, his negligence endangered Samantha. Burrowing his face in her silky hair, he held her so fiercely she began to squirm.

"Too much love, Lo Lo, too much."

"Sorry, princess. Your ma's waiting for you and Alexis, too." Holding her close but not so tightly, he took her to Meg.

Meg had been quiet through the episode, afraid to move, fearing any move would be wrong. In the sudden stillness, she could only look at the beloved, dark head bent over Samantha's and offer prayers of thanksgiving. The numbing fear receded, and she wanted to throw her arms around both of them and hold on. She took one step forward before the stark, condemning mask of Shiloh's face stopped her.

"She's fine, Meg. No thanks to any of us but Dakota." He put the child in her arms, his hand resting longer than necessary on Samantha's head. Drawing a ragged breath he spun and walked hurriedly away.

Clutching her child to her breast, her lips resting on a downy temple, Meg stared after him. After loving her so tenderly how could he walk away now, coldly aloof and ominously erect? This was a time for rejoicing, for sharing, yet she saw anger in him so savage it was frightening.

"Someone's nodding off."

"What?" Meg had forgotten Alexis.

"Samantha's falling asleep."

It was true. After the excitement Samantha had wrapped her arms around Meg's neck, snuggled into her shoulder and settled into a drowsy half slumber. "She must be exhausted. I wonder how..."

"We can reconstruct what happened later," Alexis interrupted. "Then the recriminations can begin.

Right now, I think our little wanderer would do best in her bed.''

''You're right, of course,'' Meg agreed and followed her from the barn. Despite his strange mood Meg expected to find Shiloh waiting for her. Instead Jeb was there, with a small contingent of his security patrol and a few curious guests.

''Ladies and gentlemen.'' Jeb spoke to the crowd. ''As you can see we've had a little excitement. It's over now and no one was harmed. I'd appreciate it if you would go back to your rooms as quietly as you can.'' He faced Meg and Alexis. ''The same goes for you. You've both been through a lot tonight. We'll go through the service entrance to avoid questions.''

''Shiloh?'' Meg had to ask.

''He took a walk to clear his head,'' Jeb said.

''He's getting ready to make *our* heads roll,'' an anonymous man predicted. ''We all missed the boat tonight.''

In the distance, beneath a low-hanging oak, a cigarette glowed. Meg knew it was Shiloh. In all the weeks she'd known him she had never seen him smoke. She hadn't known that he did.

''Meg,'' Jeb said in a low voice. ''You aren't dressed for this outing. We should go before you freeze.''

Meg had forgotten she wore only Shiloh's shirt and no shoes. The morning was not cool, but she was grateful for Jeb's tact, ''Will someone see to Dakota?''

"Shiloh will rub him down and turn him out to pasture. If you ladies would come with me."

Trudging behind Jeb, Meg looked back at the shadowy oak for one more glimpse of Shiloh. The cigarette glowed again, moving to his lips and then away. He seemed distant. Different. With a sinking feeling she admitted she knew very little about the man she loved.

The fully risen sun was streaming through Meg's window when Alexis tapped at her open door. "May I come in?"

Meg looked up from her careful perusal of her empty hands. "Of course, Alexis."

"The boys are going to the pool with Jeb so they won't wake Samantha. Could I talk to you?"

Meg's gaze strayed to the crib, visible from her seat. Samantha was a pink lump beneath the tumble of her toys. "If you'd like," she said dully.

"I'm not sure where to begin." For the first time the self-composed woman seemed uncertain. Her normally vibrant skin was as pale as her hair. "I know I let you down."

"That's not true, Alexis. I've been sitting here most of the morning trying to sort it out in my mind. This was my responsibility." Meg lifted a hand to forestall the younger woman's protest. "Hear me out. Samantha obviously woke and came to me. When I wasn't here, she went looking."

"No!" Alexis interjected rapidly before Meg could stop her a second time. "She was looking for Joe. I talked to her a little while ago. She was half asleep but she asked if we could go look for him again. Meg, I don't think Samantha ever knew you weren't here. She woke. The bird was gone. She went to find him. That's all."

"Then the only mystery is how she managed her little excursion, isn't it?" There was a tinge of sarcasm in her words—nothing could be more complicated, or more obscure. It was ironic that each of them was seeking the blame while absolving the other. Meg would always remember that Alexis hadn't pointed an accusing finger. She could do it herself, quite well. "I wonder if we'll ever know how she got the chair to the door, or the lock undone?

"The service door is too heavy for her, but why didn't someone see her in the lobby? The path to the barn is long and dark; how did she have the courage to follow it? How did the sentries miss her? So many questions without answers." The smile that trembled on her lips failed to reach her eyes. "It's an old story, isn't it? Children accomplishing more than anticipated."

"I should have heard her." Alexis was adamant. "It's my job."

"The carpet's too thick. You couldn't hear her footsteps, or the scrape of the chair she dragged to the door. Maybe you sensed something. Something that made you check the children."

"You aren't angry with me?"

Meg rose from her chair and crossed to her. Laying her hand on Alexis's arm she said, "How could I be angry? You acted wisely from the beginning. You got someone to stay with the boys, sent Jeb for Shiloh, then you went looking for Samantha yourself. I'll never forget that you went in with Dakota, risking your life for her. Never! This was a comedy of errors that could've been tragic. They weren't. Let's dwell on our good fortune, not on placing blame."

Alexis covered Meg's hand where it rested. "Thank you." There was a glitter in her eyes as she rushed to change the mood of their talk. "If you're going to be here with Samantha, I'll relieve Jeb. The twins are becoming such good swimmers they'll wear him down."

Meg laughed, relieved that her sons had slept through the night's ordeal and amused at the idea they could tire Jeb Lattimer. "We wouldn't want poor Jeb exhausted, would we? Go on down. I'll be here with Samantha. When she wakes I'll bring her for a swim, too. Later, it might be a wise idea to collect Joe from the music room. Shiloh put him there for the duration of the storm."

Alexis pretended to shudder. "I heard him sing down a storm once. It was enough."

"So I'm told. Now scat. Jeb might be needing you."

Meg's smile faded as Alexis left her. Would she could follow her own advice. Forget last night and not dwell on it. Samantha's escape from the inn was amazing. The greatest truth was that she and she alone would have been to blame for any harm that might have come to her child. Like a cat in heat she had gone to Shiloh, succumbing to her desire. Like the strumpet she'd played, she reaped what she deserved.

There was hatred in him at dawn; she had seen it in his eyes. Soon she must face that hatred. She couldn't hide in her room forever.

Shiloh stepped from the shower when he heard the knock at his door. "This is getting to be a habit," he groaned. He wanted to ignore it. It was late and he hadn't slept in over thirty-six hours. Granted, it was his fault. No one had forced him to ride with the storm; nor to sit by his bed watching Meg as she slept. He could blame no one for his idiocy but himself.

"Coming," he grumbled. He strode across the room while trying to wrap a sodden towel around his waist. Irritable and angry, he flung the door open without looking up from his task. "Look, Jeb," he said through gritted teeth. "I know I said to call me if anything happened but..." He stopped, sighing heavily. "You're not Jeb."

Meg was nervous. It had taken her hours to gather enough courage to take the endless walk across the hall. "I should've called first, but I was afraid you wouldn't see me."

"Why would I not?" She looked so frightened he wanted to draw her to him and promise there was nothing to fear. But he'd already proven his promises were empty shells.

"You've been avoiding me. You didn't come to the pool when the children were swimming. You skipped lunch and dinner. I had no choice but to come to you here."

"What reason would I have to avoid you?" His voice was jeering. He hated the sound of it himself.

Meg recoiled before that hard, cold face, and only the memory of a gentler man allowed her to continue. "We've always been truthful with each other, I think. Let's keep that part between us at least." Yes, Meg thought, we've been truthful. I said I loved you. You never said it. Not once. That was your truth, and I didn't understand.

An elderly guest walked past, glancing casually at them. Her second incredulous look at the nearly naked man towering over the small pale woman drew a gasp. With a shake of her blue-tinted head and a sound suspiciously like a chuckle she hurried away.

"This discussion isn't necessary, but if you insist on having it we'd better conduct it somewhere other than the hall." He stood aside, gesturing her in, convinced he'd lost his mind. Meg seemed unaware of his state of undress and his physical response to her, but Mrs. Holcomb certainly wasn't. "I was just getting out of the shower. If you'll excuse me, I'll get dressed."

Meg tried not to let him disturb her and failed miserably. From her first glance, though she kept her eyes riveted on his face, she was conscious of him. Not as the exasperated, half dressed male who glared down at her, but as the magnificently tender lover he'd been. Last night she had touched and caressed him, her body fitting his like a glove. In the enchantment he had whispered sweet, wonderful things to her. Now, because he wanted it, she must pretend it meant nothing.

As he turned from her she was barely able to stifle a cry of distress. There were new marks across his back and over his ribs, raw evidence of their mad rush to the barn through the thick underbrush. Limbs had clawed at her, but his shirt had protected her. Though Shiloh had worn no shirt, she was certain he could have avoided most of his injuries had he not shielded her instead.

His wounds needed more care than he could give them, but she dared not offer her help. He would accept nothing from her. That rare, beautiful trust they'd shared was lost.

"Will I ever understand you, Shiloh?" she said to the empty room, and the walls seemed to echo with silence.

Shiloh dressed in a sweat suit and, sitting on his bed, slid his feet into canvas deck shoes. Meg was waiting, but he did not rise. With a sigh he buried his face in his hands. His head hurt, his body hurt, his heart hurt. In twenty-four hours he had come full circle. For awhile last night he had thought…no, he had believed that there was more in this life for him than loneliness. Meg brought him love. All he'd had to do was reach for it. And dear God, it had been wonderful! But he was greedy and thoughtless, and an innocent child almost paid the cost of his reckless passion.

He knew then that Meg couldn't be his. For ten

years he'd been little more than a caged animal. Now he was a stranger in the civilized world. Somewhere in the struggle to survive he had forgotten how to love. In learning again he would hurt her over and over. Eventually she would come to hate him. It was better she hated him now.

He rose then. If he'd thought he'd been hurt before, he knew now he was wrong. But what he was about to do had to be. He crossed his room with slow, reluctant steps. As he entered the sitting room he felt a wave of disgust at himself for the innocence he would soon destroy. He had taken Meg's love and now he was going to turn it into a cheap one-night stand. When he was done she would feel dirty and used, and love would be hate.

"All right, Meg," he said with an air of impatience, taking the seat across from her. "Suppose you tell me what you feel you must say."

"I came to thank you for saving Samantha's life, and I came to apologize." She was subdued and fragile in his oversize chair.

Shiloh tried not to compare this Meg with the vibrant, glowing woman who had held him, hurt for him and given herself to him without reservation, while expecting nothing in return for the treasure she offered. The radiance was dimmed, her generous spirit crushed. In the end she had taken nothing away from their night, nothing but grief and disappointment.

His gaze fell to the ring on her right hand. She'd been hurt by the weakness of one man. The ring was proof she'd never recovered. He wouldn't be the second to hurt her, at least no more than he had already. With more tenderness than he intended he said, "You have nothing to apologize for, Meg."

"I have everything to apologize for." An obdurate note sounded in her voice. She clung to it for the strength she needed. "I shouldn't have involved you in our lives. We've cost you dearly. You've worked day and night, exhausted and in pain.

"If it weren't for us you would've gone to see for yourself that Gabe was all right. I know how you worried about all of them. Worst of all, I almost cost you your most precious possession. Because of me you nearly destroyed Dakota." There were tears brimming in her eyes, but Meg was made of strong stock. Swallowing hard she continued. "I've always thought I was a good mother."

"Meg." There was a painful cramp in his throat, and his eyes ached like hot coals. He found he couldn't quite stand coolly by while she tore herself apart. "Don't do this."

She shivered violently, sending the long curl at her shoulder tumbling down her back. "Don't stop me, please. I have to say this and I can only do it this once. This morning I was criminally careless. You saved my daughter's life—and mine, too, because I don't know what would've become of me if I'd lost her."

He wanted to tell her again that none of this was needed. That the blame was his, not hers. Instead he kept his painful silence and let her speak.

"Last night was a mistake. You tried to send me away. I wouldn't listen and I'm sorry. I can't ask you to forget the trouble I've caused, but I hope someday you can forgive me."

"There's nothing to forgive," he said honestly. Then he launched into his abominable lie. "We shared a good time, as people who are attracted to each other often do. It was just one of those things that happen for no rhyme or reason." He wanted to close his eyes and shut out the sight of her stricken face, but he wouldn't let himself off that easily. If he was going to hurt her, he would see it and he would feel it, and he would live with it forever. "We babbled a lot of nonsense and, at the worst, we were carelessly selfish. The result was almost tragic, but things turned out for the best. It's over. Samantha's safe. Soon we'll find Ballenger and deal with him. Then you can go home and forget you've ever heard of me."

Shiloh saw that each word hit her like a sledgehammer as he reduced the most wonderful night in his life to cheap lust. He searched her face for the hate that would make it easier. He saw only despair.

Meg stared at him but she could hardly see him. She knew he was angry, but she hadn't expected this brutal coldness. Each word cut deeper into her until there was a block of ice where her heart had been. She was no longer a warm-blooded woman who had pulsed with the magic of love. She was a robot functioning as programmed. Why else hadn't she fallen, mortally wounded, at his feet?

''If it were only myself I must consider I'd leave tomorrow. I can't do that to the children.'' She spoke woodenly as if by rote. The wonder was that she could speak at all. ''This is the only safe place for them.''

She turned her blank eyes from him, her hand twisting the corded side of her slacks. *Nonsense!* Those tender, loving words he'd whispered, never that he loved her, but loving all the same, had been a sated man's trivia. Her fingers nervously closed over her leg like a vise as she struggled with a rising sickness.

The silence between them was thick and black. There was blood on Shiloh's lips as he fought the need to kneel at her feet and take her in his arms, sweeping into oblivion the lies he spoke. He couldn't. He'd gone too far for second thoughts. What he'd done couldn't be undone. He was setting her free of the hurt he might bring her. That should have made it easier...but it didn't. Wearily he leaned back, watching her, his hands clenched into a single punishing fist pressed against his bloody lips.

Stilling her fingers, Meg grasped at a shred of dignity. ''Stonebridge has been good for the boys. They'd like to kidnap Joe when we go. They've missed the beginning of kindergarten, but Alexis and I are teaching them.'' She stopped short realizing she had begun to ramble. ''I'm sorry, I don't know where that came from. It doesn't concern you.''

''Meg.'' He waited until her downcast eyes met

his. "I'm glad the children have liked it here. My home is yours for as long as you need it."

"Thank you, Shiloh...for everything." Because she had no voice for more she rose.

"Meg."

She stopped on her way to the door but didn't turn to him. Her shoulders hunched as if she expected one more blow. Shiloh thought he would die of shame. Hoarsely he said, "I *will* keep you safe from Ballenger. In that I won't fail."

She relaxed. That dark river of hair he loved so much swayed with her silent nod and she hurried from the room.

From his seat, through the open door, he watched her cross the hall. Her body was shaking. She walked with the careful step of an old woman. God! What had he done to her?

With the flat of his hand he raked the top of the table before him, sending a small, perfect carving of a wild duck and a rare, primitive bowl filled with flowers crashing against the wall. His smile was empty, his voice bitter. "Thank you, Shiloh!"

The words echoed over and over in his head and he knew then he would kill any man who did to Meg what he had just done.

"Not hungry, Mom?"

"What, Tommy?" Meg looked up from the salad she toyed with.

"He said aren't you hungry." Eddie's face wore the same worried look as his brother's.

"I guess I had too much lunch." Meg tried to assume a cheerful expression as she pushed her plate away.

Each evening for the past week, the twins asked to dine in the small garden café by the pool. The days were growing shorter and lanterns lining the walks gave the alcove a festive look. Like a party, Tommy had declared. The garden at dusk was pleasant, but the real attractions were Shiloh and Dakota, riding the rough trails by the river.

Meg suffered the meals in silence, never daring to lift her eyes from the table. One glance at Shiloh and she knew she would break, as she did each night in the solitude of her room.

The routine never varied. At twilight Shiloh and Dakota thundered from the meadow like Bellerophon and Pegasus, and Meg's agony began. With her face pale, her eyes clouded by shadows of fatigue, she watched as the full moon began to rise. She went aimlessly through the motions of her evenings: time with the children, an hour or two at her drawing board and finally a hot shower that did nothing for her aching body. In her sleepless bed she lay rigid, waiting for his weary footsteps and the muted click of his door. Another brutal ride ended. He was safe! Then her silent tears would begin to fall.

Dakota's jubilant whinny floated from the meadow, jolting Meg to the present. She ached in every muscle, and every nerve was finely drawn. To her horror tears threatened early. In a strained voice she spoke to the boys. "I know you'd looked forward to the chocolate parfait, but I'd like to check on your sister."

It wasn't completely a lie. Samantha hadn't felt well during the afternoon, not quite feverish, but cranky as if she might be soon. "We'll order double parfaits from room service."

"Alexis, too?" Eddie asked.

"Well, maybe not a double for Alexis and me, but certainly a little one." Meg had no idea of the troubled gazes following her through the garden. To guests who came to the inn annually for golf and tennis or bridge, it was apparent something had gone terribly wrong. The unhappiness in their host and the lovely young widow was almost palpable.

"A pity," Mrs. Holcomb clucked to the ladies at her table.

"Enough!" Jeb Lattimer muttered only to himself. Tossing aside his napkin, he rose from his solitary table. Instead of trailing Meg as was his custom, he turned toward the meadow. His hurried stride was angry as he moved to intercept Shiloh in his rampage over the countryside. As horse and rider sped by he stepped through a hedge, catching the reins, using his considerable size to bring Dakota to a rearing halt.

"What the hell!" Shiloh quieted the horse and glared at Jeb. "Are you trying to kill yourself?"

"Are you?" Jeb stared up at Shiloh. "Riding at night is insanity at the best of times, and these aren't the best of times for you. You aren't sleeping; you aren't eating. When you aren't trying to break your neck on this damn stallion you're walking the grounds. We have more than enough people to do that. Competent people.''

''Who let a child wander at the mercy of God knows what. We were lucky it was only Dakota and a rattler she met.'' Shiloh jerked the reins from Jeb's hand.

''Dammit, Shiloh.'' Jeb grabbed his arm, nearly unseating him. ''You've been punishing yourself. Meg's been punishing herself. You act like strangers, when any fool knows you're much more.'' Shiloh pulled his arm away slowly, cold, blue eyes glowering down into tawny eyes.

Jeb refused to be intimidated. He'd waited days to have his say, and have it he would. ''I didn't have to find you two together to know you were going to be lovers if you weren't already. Hell, everybody at the inn has known it. It's been written all over both of you since the day Jingo brought you here. I don't know what kind of heavy scene you're trying to play, but you're hurting your lady, and she doesn't deserve it. Damn you, man, do you know how she looks at you when you walk by as if she's invisible?''

''Jeb.'' Shiloh's jaw rippled, his teeth clenched. ''It's better this way. Things got out of hand, and I made some mistakes. Samantha almost paid for them. Ballenger will surface soon, and we'll deal with him. Then Meg can go, and I can't hurt her anymore.''

''Is that what this is all about? You're backing off because you made a mistake? Hell, we all made a mistake. Where was I when Samantha took her stroll? Where was Alexis, or the hotel staff, or anyone of this private army you've employed? You spent a fortune on surveillance, and she slipped through it. So we were lucky and nothing happened. Instead of sulking about it like a kid who found a worm in his apple you should get down on your knees and thank God that you have an apple.''

''What if it had been Ballenger? What if he had walked right in as easily?''

''He couldn't. A grown man couldn't have gone where Samantha did without detection.''

''Jeb.'' Shiloh abandoned the argument. ''I have to handle this as I see fit.''

''No matter who gets hurt? Can't the two of you get together and explain things? Meg explained to Alexis; you've explained to me. Talk to each other; you might be surprised what you hear.''

''What does that mean?'' Shiloh's eyes were like hard, blue stones.

''Don't ask me, buddy. If you get any explanations you get them from your lady.''

''She's not my lady.''

''Oh? Somehow I got the idea she thought she was.''

''Why would she think that?''

''She's not exactly the type to go to bed with a man unless she loved him. Even you can't be that big a fool. Why don't you tell her how she failed the test, she deserves that much. Just as it would be kinder to shoot Dakota in his stall than to ruin him on a dark hillside.''

''You can be a real bastard, Jeb.''

''I took lessons from the master.'' Jeb stepped away from Dakota, lifted his hands in a final gesture and walked away.

Shiloh slumped in the saddle. The truth hurt, but perhaps one day Jeb would understand some things weren't meant to be.

''Not for me,'' he said and with a gentleness that surprised him, he urged Dakota toward the trail.

Nine

"Another false lead!" Shiloh slammed the report he was reading down on his desk. "Ballenger is everywhere and nowhere."

He felt the weight of Jeb Lattimer's level gaze. For ten days they had observed a truce. Though Shiloh heeded Jeb's wisdom, ceasing the savage night rides, neither apologized. Jeb's single reference to the incident was a terse, "The horse doesn't know any better. You do." And Shiloh knew he spoke of more than riding.

Shiloh picked up his papers again, but his thoughts were on Jeb. Once Gabe had predicted that if he hurt Caroline, her scar-faced friend would cut out his heart and feed it to the vultures. Shiloh suspected Jeb would gladly inflict the same fate on him.

''You're very fond of Meg, aren't you?'' He broke the strained silence that fell between them far too frequently.

''She's a classy lady.'' Jeb, his expression guarded, obviously wondered where this was leading. The subject of Meg had been off limits since his outburst.

''I asked if you were fond of her.''

''Yeah.'' Jeb laid his reports aside. ''Fond enough not to like what you're doing to her.''

''You've never made a move. There were opportunities.''

Jeb snorted indelicately. ''Only for you, my friend. I was tempted, but I don't have to be hit over the head to recognize the truth. At least Mama Lattimer didn't raise no fools.''

The last was a slow drawl with the sting of an insult. Shiloh held his temper. He couldn't afford to be angry with Jeb. He needed him. Ignoring the barb he said with a studied calm, ''When this is over, there will be difficult adjustments, some healing. Would you see her through it?''

''That's your job, not mine.''

''No.'' Shiloh's hands were clasped on the desk, and the knotted muscles of his forearms betrayed his stress. ''I forfeited that privilege.''

''Dammit!'' Jeb shouted. ''One mistake doesn't mean the end of the world. Meg doesn't blame you. She lo—''

''As a favor to me, Jeb?''

''She wouldn't need me if you'd just—''

''As my friend,'' Shiloh continued implacably.

"Lord." Jeb rolled his eyes heavenward. "Deliver me from stubborn idiots." He sighed heavily, running his fingers through thick, golden hair. "All right. As a friend, but—"

"Thanks, Jeb," Shiloh said softly. "I'll owe you."

"Not me," Jeb grumbled. "You don't owe *me* a thing."

Shiloh turned his attention to the papers, conscious that neither of them considered the consequences of failure. He wouldn't fail! Not a second time. He scanned the reports, searching for a clue he knew was not there. His frustration spilled over. "There's nothing new on Ballenger's family?"

"There's nothing to report. They're cooperating."

"Are they?" A distorted brow lifted.

"They're good people. They love Evan, but they see him as a changeling who's never fit into the family. They'll do whatever it takes to stop him from hurting anyone else."

"We can't be certain of that."

"I am. They weren't responsible for what their son did any more than Meg was responsible for Keith's criminal drunkenness, but they'll make what amends they can. By helping us."

Shiloh tossed the reports aside, absently massaging his throbbing temple. His shoulder slumped, and his voice was half apologetic. "I suppose you're right. Ballenger's family is as much the victim as Meg's."

"I know I'm right." Jeb leaped to his feet. "Meg," he exclaimed. "What brings you to our lair?"

Shiloh spun his chair slowly toward the door,

dreading what the sight of her would do to him, but hungry for it. She waited, framed by the dark wood, beautiful and fragile with a tensile strength beneath. How many crises had she endured, each more destructive than the last? The toll was mounting. It was tallied in her taut face, the defensive brace of her shoulders.

Her eyes were huge, their haunting color luminous. Her hair was slicked back severely with a clasp at her nape. Shiloh wanted to set it free, winding it in his hands, binding her to him. He wanted to kiss those somber lips until they were swollen and contented with his loving. He wanted to touch the slender body his hands had caressed. He wanted…

A muscle rippled in his jaw, and his lips curled in disgust. It didn't matter what he wanted.

Jeb threw him a look, questioning his silence, then shrugged. ''Is something wrong, Meg?''

''Nothing,'' she said quickly. ''I need to speak with Shiloh.''

Jeb moved to the door. ''I have things to do; we can finish this later.''

''Don't go!'' Meg cried, grasping at Jeb's arm.

She's afraid to be alone with me, Shiloh thought. His heart constricted. No pain had ever been like this. He should say something, set her at ease, but what?

After another expectant pause, Jeb assumed the burden of conversation. ''Come, sit down.''

''There's no need. This won't take long.'' She hid her shaking hands behind her. ''I've decided the children and I should leave.'' Her eyes closed in relief.

It was done. With more confidence she added, ''It's time we went home.''

''No!'' Shiloh's flinty voice lashed out.

Meg's eyelids fluttered open, her gaze meeting his for the first time, refusing to be intimidated. She couldn't argue. He was too strong, too persuasive. She would simply state her case and go. ''There's been no sign of Ballenger for weeks. Maybe his threat was an empty one and he's just disappeared. He could be dead.'' She flung her hands in emphasis. ''I can't stay here forever waiting for...for whatever. The children need to get on with their lives. We need to go home.''

''You can't!''

''I can.''

''It isn't safe.''

''With Sheriff Martin's protection it will be.''

''No!'' Shiloh said bitterly, his gaze dueling with hers.

''We can't hide all our lives.'' She looked to Jeb for help, but with a shrug he excluded himself from their contest of wills. Meg's stomach knotted, an omen of defeat. In quiet despair she said, ''We have to go.''

She expected his voice to lash at her again, but suddenly all the fire drained from him. ''Give me a week.'' His bleak voice was almost pleading. ''If we haven't found Ballenger by then, I'll let you go.''

Meg's heart somersaulted beneath the tight band that crushed her chest. He sounded as if it was the last thing he wanted...as if he wanted her to stay...wanted her! Dear heaven, if it was true she would stay forever. But he wasn't asking for forever. Tears were close; she must end this soon. "All right." She couldn't fight him, not when he looked at her with that sad, lost expression. "A week. If there's no word by then the children and I will leave."

"Thank you," he said simply and fell silent. Another word and he would be on his feet, taking her in his arms, and if he did, he would never let her go.

A futile hollowness filled him. The darkness of incomparable loss. A wordless echo of a lonely cry. He felt their eyes on him. Jeb's puzzled, angry. Meg's hurt, glistening, her defiance broken. Because something more was needed, he heard himself say in a voice that had little resemblance to his, "I'll contact Sheriff Martin. Seven days should be enough to prepare for your homecoming."

She left him then, without a word, her small figure moving bravely away. She was gone from his sight but never his memory. He remembered a woman, unbelievably lovely, wrapped in a gown of blue-green fire, touching him, holding him, whispering that she loved him. He remembered the stricken look in her eyes when she confided she might have conceived a child. *His child*...a child she hadn't known could never be...and she had been afraid.

"Afraid of me," he mused. "For me."

"She's right." Jeb interrupted his muttering in an odd tone. "She can't spend her life hiding."

Shiloh looked at him blankly. He'd forgotten Jeb. "I'm asking for a week, not a lifetime."

"When you're hurting, a week *is* a lifetime. Either

love the woman and be thankful for the privilege, or let her go."

"I can't." His face was a tortured mask. "Not yet. There's never been a woman who mattered. Never love. No one in three years. Since I first saw her." He rambled, his barely coherent thoughts a startling revelation. There was hell in the blue gaze that finally met Jeb's. "I don't know how to love her."

"There's no trick to it," Jeb said in a broken rumble. "You simply open your heart and follow its lead."

"I could hurt her again."

"I'd wager all I have that your lady would rather risk being hurt by you than live without you."

"My lady," Shiloh said softly.

"Yeah, your lady. Think about it. What it's going to be like when she's gone. You've got a week to come to your senses and grab the brass ring. Start thinking about it right now. I've got to touch base with the men. I'll be back in half an hour."

Without Jeb the office was eerily quiet. The stream of activity had miraculously stopped. Shiloh closed his aching eyes and let himself dream of Meg and what might have been.

In the sanctuary of her room Meg leaned her head against the window pane. How many times had she stood here, her courage ebbing, with only the cool glass to soothe her? How many times had she found contentment in a sunrise or sunset, or hoped for a stolen glimpse of Shiloh?

''Masochist,'' she muttered. Why she did punish herself with reminders of what she'd never have? He'd asked for a week. Seven days and she'd never see him again. She shivered, rubbing her arms, telling herself it was the chill of fall. Lifting her head she concentrated on the changing world before her. It was different now, with a wash of warm, rich color threading through the evergreen. Leaves that murmured softly in the summer wind rustled crisply, like the chatter of gossiping geese. The season had changed. She had changed.

Glancing at her unfinished manuscript she winced. A deadline drew near but work that had once gone splendidly had come to a halt. Creativity shriveled to nothing as she mooned around like a lovesick teenager with only Shiloh on her mind.

''A week will change that.'' The room rang with her conviction. She would put Ballenger and Shiloh from her mind, and end the paralysis of this uncertain limbo. Shiloh's charitable hospitality was stretched to the breaking point, and she had a living to earn. Though the children were learning under Alexis's tutelage and her own, it wasn't the same as formal kindergarten. They were happy here, happier than they'd ever been, but they could be happy in Lawndale. With Sheriff Martin's help they would be safe.

I'll be happier, too, she promised fiercely. Lonelier, emptier, duller, she admitted, but happier. An irrevocable truth seized her mind. *I have loved Shiloh, a man like no other. My life will never be the same.*

But in Lawndale she could ease the hurt, pretend

she'd dreamed the man who made love to her. She could fool herself into believing those cherished moments had never happened. In her old life there would be nothing to trigger memories of a night that now lived in the ashes of her pride. She could forget the crispness of his hair beneath her fingertips, the virile scent of him, the imprint of his body that marked hers for all time.

For a little while she could forget that her heart and body belonged to Shiloh and always would. Even though he didn't want them.

The sound at her door was a cross between a scratch and a tap. Meg was sorely tempted to ignore it, but thoughts of her children forbade it. To her surprise it wasn't her brood and their keeper but a tall, elderly lady she'd seen at the bridge tables constantly for weeks. She searched for a name. "Mrs. Holcomb?"

The old lady inclined her head regally. "My dear, I wouldn't normally intrude, but I was in the florist's shop today when a rather brash young man approached me. He knew I was a guest at the inn, I suppose, from the van that took us on our excursion. He asked about you, said he was a friend, that he wanted to surprise you with these." From behind her she produced a small bouquet of carnations. "I wouldn't usually act as a delivery person, but you've looked so sad of late, and the flowers were pretty. I hope you enjoy the bouquet and will forgive my presumption." She pressed the flowers into Meg's hands and hurried away.

"Who would send me flowers?" For a mad moment she thought of Shiloh and knew she was being ridiculous. Closing the door behind her she drew the card from its envelope. The scrawled initials jumped out at her. E.B. Evan Ballenger!

"He's in the village." She swayed on her feet, crushing the flowers against her. She recognized the brittle edge of panic in her voice, and with a strength she hadn't known she had she made herself think. She read the message carefully and more than once before its meaning registered.

He had her children! That flowing, girlish script with its evil message meant they were in danger.

"It's not true." She flung the hated bouquet and the card from her. The children had gone to the village library with Alexis as they did every Tuesday. Shiloh had been persuaded to allow this treat and it was one she usually shared. Today she'd stayed behind to lay the groundwork for their departure.

Meg looked at her bedside clock. It was four. They were always back by three. "They're in the music room. Alexis was going to teach them some new songs." She spoke in a stilted tone, convincing herself. "I'll go there, and they'll be fine."

Shattering the flowers under her heel, she ran from the room. Oblivious of stares and comments, she raced through the hall and down the stairs as if Satan himself were behind her. At the music room, before its open door, she stopped. It was empty.

"Oh, God!" she whimpered. "He has my babies." As she sagged in anguish, from deep inside her a wiser self commanded, *Think!* "Yes, yes, I have to think." Grasping her head with her hands she racked her mind for the instructions in the message. "The quarry. Alone. No one must know." She parroted words feverishly as bits of the note became whole.

"Mrs. Sullivan?" Tim, the bellboy, leaned over her. "Are you ill?"

"What?" Meg lifted her head from her hands, grasping at the excuse he offered. "A headache! That's it. It came on so quickly it startled me."

"Can I get you an aspirin? Shall I call Mr. Butler?"

"No!" she said too abruptly. "A walk in the fresh air is what I need."

"You're sure?"

"Very sure." Meg tried a smile. "It's better already, but I'll take that walk for insurance."

She made herself walk decorously through the lobby and the grounds. At the garden's edge, she checked carefully to be certain no one observed. Fortune was with her. Carl, the guard for this sector, had looked away. Thankful for this small bit of luck she slipped through the thicket and into the shadows. Then she was running, her cautions cast aside. Running through a forest thick with fear. Hoping, praying she wouldn't be too late.

"Shiloh," Jeb said as he hurried into the office. "I just spoke with Alexis. They were delayed at the library. She called Meg then, and tried again just now from the lobby. No answer either time. Tim saw Meg near the music room, and Carl spotted her in the garden, now she's not anywhere.'' A sense of *malaise* seized Shiloh as he waited for Jeb to continue. ''One of Alexis's tires was slashed. It looked like an accident, but now Meg has disappeared.'' A worried amber gaze met Shiloh's. ''I don't like this one damn bit.''

''Send someone to her room, fast,'' Shiloh instructed. Then, pushing his chair back and tossing his pen aside, he countered, ''No! I'll go.''

The telephone on his desk rang. He hesitated, then lifted it impatiently. ''Butler,'' he barked into the receiver, anxious to be away. The voice on the line was dreadfully familiar. His rush subsided. He sank into his chair, his hand at his forehead, shielding his face. His questions had the rapid fire of a machine gun. ''When? How? How long?'' Then, despondent, ''Yeah, luck. And thanks, Sheriff Martin.''

''Ballenger!''

''He's on his way here—if he isn't here already.'' Shiloh's skin was drawn tightly over his face, pulling down the scarred corner of his left eye.

''How?''

''A neighbor of Meg's, a Miss Hillyard, recalled a stranger asking questions. Where she was, who she was with.''

''She couldn't know.''

''She asked him to tea and talked her head off. Amazingly she remembered me from the funeral and, dammit, thought she'd seen me at Meg's later.''

Jeb sucked a long breath through his teeth. ''I suppose Ballenger got a perfect description of you.''

''Worse. Sheriff Martin says she's a sweet old busybody who never forgets a face or a name.''

''Bingo! The name Shiloh Butler isn't exactly unknown. Tracing you will be child's play. At least she reported the nice, curious stranger.''

''Two days after the fact,'' Shiloh said levelly.

''Damn!'' Jeb exploded. ''I'll alert the men and bring Alexis and the children to the room. You see to Meg.'' He paused at the door. ''If there's anything good about this it's that it's almost over. Meg couldn't take much more.''

Her door was open. Shiloh stepped inside, bending to pick up the crushed bouquet. Flowers from an admirer? He'd never given her flowers. Perhaps he never would. His eyes wandered over the orderly clutter of her room, seeking a clue that would indicate where she'd gone.

He touched the yellow cotton gown tossed over the foot of the bed, remembering that once she'd come to him in a gown as fine as the morning mist. He breathed the subtle scent that clung to it, holding it in his lungs, a small part of her that could be his.

The white card was caught under the convoluted runner of a bentwood rocker. ''What the devil?'' he muttered as he retrieved it. The message hit him like an earthquake, and he sank into the chair, struggling with fear.

She had gone to Ballenger because of a clever

hoax, the product of a mad, brilliant mind. Ballenger couldn't infiltrate the security of the inn, so he hadn't tried. Instead, with a foolproof lure he had drawn her into his trap. How had he managed the flowers? A half remembered image swam in Shiloh's mind. Mrs. Holcomb bustling across the lobby with a bouquet of flowers. *This* bouquet.

"Damn you, Ballenger!" He threw them against the wall. "Harm her and I'll kill you with my bare hands."

His control was icy and deadly when he went to Meg's telephone. His first call was to Cass, the stable master. Dakota would be saddled and waiting, with a loaded rifle in the scabbard. The second call was to Jeb.

"I've had the children put in a different room," Jeb reported. "No one but security knows where. Alexis won't leave them. The guards are posted as planned. The service stair has been barred."

"Good." With the children carefully guarded he could give his full concentration to Meg. Thanks to Jeb, the black-sheep son of a prominent family. Whatever he was or was not, their association had been strong and successful and as personally rewarding as it was lucrative. He could count on Jeb as he would his right hand. "I'm taking Dakota. We'll shortcut through the forest."

"I put a call in to Jingo. We're in luck. He's in the vicinity. He'll be here in less than ten minutes."

"How did you know we'd need him?"

"I didn't. I was just covering all the bases to keep

Meg safe. Take care, Shiloh. Jingo and I will be right behind you."

Shiloh couldn't speak his gratitude. He didn't try. He simply dropped the telephone receiver and ran.

Cass was waiting with Dakota. The rifle was in place, and alongside it, a knife. Neither Cass nor Shiloh bothered with words. Shiloh mounted, leaned down to grip and release Cass's hand, then spurred Dakota into a gallop.

Their night rides reaped a dividend. They had ranged the land from river to quarry and back again. Shiloh gave Dakota his head, letting him dodge trees and leap gullies at breakneck speed. All he need do was hold on.

Near the quarry he drew Dakota to a halt. Though his heart urged him to rush to Meg, his head commanded caution. Ballenger would be like a wounded animal, unpredictable, cunning and doubly dangerous.

"Whoa, boy." He soothed the horse as he studied the rim of the quarry. It was too quiet. Nothing moved. "Easy," he whispered as Dakota flicked his ears. "I know he's here." Sweat trickled down Shiloh's face and into his eyes, but he dare not wipe it away.

"Where are you, Meg?" he muttered. "Make a move, give me some sign. You knew I'd come."

Far in the distance he heard the pounding of chopper blades cutting the air. Jingo was flying the machine like a demon, low and hard and fast.

Suddenly a gaunt figure sprang from a fold in the red dirt. His eyes were banked with the blinding fire of madness as he shook a challenging fist toward the offending noise from the sky. Shiloh had seen eyes like that only once before. They were eyes lost in the pits of hell, smoldering in the face of a mass murderer.

Muted agony ripped at Shiloh's throat. He knew he was too late. What Ballenger intended had been done. Meg's one chance, if there was one, was the quarry. As the lesser of evils, Shiloh prayed the madman had thrown her into its murky depths. Hypothermia would be rapid, but still it gave him hope, it bought her time.

Time! They'd had so little. It was so precious. A battle cry tore from him as he spurred Dakota forward, a cry of anguish for a love that might be lost.

Ballenger froze. Dazedly he turned his eyes from the sky. Shiloh could have ridden him down; he wanted to, but some primitive instinct warned that if he was to have a life with Meg it mustn't be tainted with murder.

The lanky man turned to run a step too late. Shiloh launched himself from the saddle, rolling with his prey, their fall knocking the breath from their bodies. Ballenger clawed at Shiloh's face, kicked at his legs, screaming like a hysterical animal as they rolled in the dust. Long, thin arms were everywhere, coiling with the serpentine strength of insanity. Together they tumbled, sprawling over shrub and stone. Shiloh managed a solid punch and another. Ballenger's screaming stopped in midcry. He was as still as he was silent.

Shuddering, Shiloh rose to his feet. Cuts and bruises marked his face and arms, but he thought only of Meg. He turned away, realizing even as he did that he couldn't go, not yet. There was a promise he must keep. The children must be kept safe. Ballenger mustn't reach them. Meg wouldn't thank him for her life if it cost theirs.

At his signal Dakota came to him. Shiloh was almost clumsy in his frantic rush. He took a loop of rope from the pommel of the saddle. Binding Ballenger's skeletal body like a mummy, he dragged it to a tree. His last act, a reflexive one, was to slap Dakota on his rump, sending him home.

"Now, Meg, now. Please..." Please what? He didn't know, but it was his prayer for her.

As if on cue Jingo came roaring over the trees. Without a backward glance Shiloh sprinted to the clearing, reaching for the dangling ladder as the craft hovered in a whirlwind of dust. Shielding his eyes Shiloh braced himself as Jingo lifted away. Airborne, the force of the blades did not reverberate off the trees, and no flying debris beat at the craft like popcorn, but Shiloh heard only bits of Jeb's shout.

"The quarry!" The rest was lost as the draft of the blades tore the words from his lips. It was enough. Meg was in the cold water of the quarry. Resorting to hand signals Jeb explained their plan. Jingo would go in as low as he dared. Once Shiloh was in the water he would hover as long as was needed. Jeb would pull them into the chopper.

It was a long shot, but it was their only chance. Jingo's helicopter was not equipped for rescue. The lives of Shiloh and Meg would depend on the skill of one, the strength of the other. Clinging to the ladder Shiloh looked into Jeb's eyes, and with a nod he put his life in the hands of his friends.

On Jeb's command Jingo dipped to strafe the water, searching. Meg was not there. Shiloh waited, every nerve frayed by agony. Suddenly she surfaced. Her hair fanning out in the water, her movements in slow motion. Hypothermia!

Shiloh plunged into the water. His fall took him deeply in the chill water. He was disoriented by the cold, then righting himself, he surged to the surface. Meg was gone. He kicked, diving, his arms reaching, flailing, struggling to find her. Nothing. He surfaced, snatched a breath to dive again and Meg was there, not more than six feet away, treading water almost forgetfully. Her skin was pallid, her lips blue. As he saw her, her motion stopped and she began to drift beneath the surface.

''Meg!'' he cried, pulling himself toward her with powerful strokes. As she slipped completely under for what he feared would be the last time, his fingertips tangled in her hair. Then his arm was around her, holding her against him. ''I have you, darling. You're safe.''

''Shiloh?'' His name was a blurred sound, her cold lips barely moved. ''Shiloh hates me.''

She was dead weight, not fully conscious. He knew she wouldn't remember, but for himself he said, ''I don't hate you, darling. I love you. Just hang on and when this is over I'll spend the rest of my life proving it.''

Holding her securely against him with one arm, he signaled his friends. The ladder skimmed the surface. The blades whipped the water to a froth, splashing Meg's face. He had to get her warm before it was too late.

He hooked the ladder with his arm, winding a leg through the rungs. Jingo wouldn't move until there was no danger of falling. Inch by inch they were drawn up, then jerked to a halt. Their weight must be too much for Jeb. Suddenly they moved again, easier. Jeb had tapped his reserves, finding an inhuman strength. Miraculously they were at the chopper and the blond giant was reaching for Shiloh. He was laughing, hauling them in as if they were weightless.

The floor was firm under Shiloh's feet. A blanket was wrapped tightly around them, and the door slammed shut before Shiloh looked at Jeb. His hands were raw and battered, the veins in his arms distended, gorged by the power of his efforts. How could he repay this man? Shiloh wondered. Before he could find his voice Jeb settled the matter.

A grin flashed in his tanned face. The look that swept Meg's bedraggled form was tender. "Okay?"

"Okay," Shiloh said softly. It was all the thanks Jeb would ever want.

"Jingo," Jeb called over the roar of the engines. "Let's take Shiloh and his lady home."

Meg whimpered, bringing Shiloh to his knees. Kneeling by her side he stroked the tangle of her hair from her face, whispering words she couldn't hear.

For hours he'd sat by her bedside as she lay still as death, the slow rise and fall of her breasts the only sign of life. Even the children hadn't roused her with their hugs and kisses. The sedative the doctor had given her held her deeply in its healing oblivion.

"Don't remember. Don't dream," he murmured, hoping shock would wipe from her memory Ballenger's glaring eyes, his fingers clawing at her throat, the still, deep water of the quarry. Shiloh shuddered, reliving the cold, his hand winding in her hair, their only lifeline as he struggled to reach her.

"Remember the good things. Jeb, giving more than even he knew he could, and Jingo, who would've flown his beloved chopper into the jaws of hell for you." His palm curved around her cheek, and his thumb traced the shape of her mouth. "Remember that I love you. You have to know I do."

Meg shivered. She spoke, but did not waken. Hoarsely she began a faltering monologue, recounting a nightmare. Each rambling word of hate and horror drove a knife into Shiloh's heart. Sliding his arms beneath her he lifted her onto his lap. With her head lying on his chest he rocked her, crooning softly over and over, "No, love. You're wrong. I don't hate you. I couldn't."

Long after she quieted he rocked her. Long after his arms lost all feeling he held her. Darkness fell and still he held her.

Shiloh sighed. His lips brushed Meg's forehead. His face was bleak. The ugliness of what he'd done to her, what he'd heard, turned him sick to his soul.

She didn't think he would come for her while she struggled alone in those dark, freezing waters. God! The despair of it. Dying, loving him as he knew she had, and thinking he didn't care.

"I cared, sweetheart. Too much to ever want to hurt you." He gathered her closer still, his lips touching her hair. "In my arrogance I decided that I alone knew what was best for you. What you wanted didn't matter. Playing God, I decided it would make it easier for you to leave me if you hated me. You had to leave me. You'd been hurt once. The ring you wear proves it. I couldn't stand to hurt you again."

With his thumb he stroked the translucent lid of her eye, marveling at the length of her sable lashes. "I threw what you brought me back in your face, to drive you away. I'm so new to loving I didn't know what I was doing was the worst thing I could do. I didn't know how it was going to hurt both of us."

Meg stirred, nestling into his arms. He knew it meant nothing, she didn't know what she did, but still his hopes rose. He cradled her like a child and told her his story. "For a long time I thought I wasn't capable of love, but now I think I've loved you since the first day I saw you. At Keith's funeral you looked right through me. You were so beautiful, so lost, and there was nothing I could do. When Ballenger escaped, in a sick way, I was almost grateful. He gave me the excuse to bring you here. I didn't know why. I just wanted you near me.

"Does it disgust you that I fed on your fear? Is that one more sin to blacken my soul? I've been a dunderheaded fool from beginning to end. Because I didn't understand that love moves beyond fear and loneliness and pain, I wanted you to hate me. And now you must. After all I've done, you couldn't love me." He swallowed and wiped a damp cheek. "If it gives you any consolation, I'll regret that the rest of my life. Some day, when this is all over, when you love someone else, perhaps you can forgive me."

The sound that came from Meg's throat was half sigh, half sob. She was tired. She needed rest, not him. She would never need him again. With a ragged breath tearing at his lungs he stood and laid her gently on her bed. Smoothing the covers over her, he kissed her cheek, whispering, "It doesn't matter. Nothing matters except that you're safe."

Rising, he stood a moment longer. He didn't want to leave her, but Alexis was close. She would hear Meg's slightest sound, and there were things he'd left undone for too long. Jeb and Jingo had been left to deal with Ballenger and the police. The inspector had been kind and patient, but he wanted to speak with him.

There was Dakota to attend to. The horse had been magnificent, as magnificent as Jeb and Jingo. Before this night ended, whether they wanted it or not, he must express his gratitude to his friends. Only then could he seek his own oblivion.

He looked down at Meg who was sleeping peacefully now. "If only..." he murmured in a strangled voice, then turned away and left her room.

Ten

By the bed a half-opened window was draped by translucent curtains. The midday sun, dulled by the cant of autumn, filtered through the curtain, touching Shiloh, warming his face, waking him with its light.

His slumber, long in coming, had been complete and deep, cleansing away the terror. He lay drowsing, half sleeping, half awake. There were aches waking too. Little ones. The soreness of a muscle that only hurt when he breathed. The sting of missing flesh, scored and guttered away by clawing nails. Spreading bruises clotted with blood and darkening. There would be more when he moved.

It didn't matter. Meg was safe. That mattered.

With his eyes closed he listened to the inn—alive, bustling, its day in full swing. He heard the walls that enclosed him creak with the furtive secrets of loneliness, and knew he was alone as he'd never been.

Somewhere close by Jingo clattered over a power line. By the barn Dakota snuffled, and Cass clucked to him. There were children playing on the lawn. Meg's children. Their laughter blended with Alexis's dulcet tones and Jeb's deep chuckle. There was a small comfort in the familiar sounds.

Ballenger was gone from their lives, no longer a threat. With this final frenzy, his schizophrenia had converted into the speechless, motionless state of catatonia. No one knew what was in his mind, or how much he remembered. But, in his netherworld, the retreat of a mind broken beyond repair, it was unlikely the Sullivans existed. The police physician had warned that recovery from catatonia, while rare, was not impossible. Shiloh remembered the thin, emaciated body, the strength that had been maniacal instead of physical. He thought of the years of forced feedings, the ultimate failure of veins to accept the IV needles, and knew that for Ballenger it was impossible. A sad ending for a sad man, who had done more damage than he could ever know.

A shout of happiness spiraled, lighthearted and contagious, rising like music in the crisp air. Eddie, with a confidence bright and new. Shiloh smiled. All was almost right with his world.

A breeze ruffled the curtain and teased the covers of his bed. Shiloh sighed, filling his lungs with the scent of jasmine and wild roses. *Meg.*

"Meg?" Dazed, like a man startled from a dream,

he rose on one elbow. The forgotten sheet slid the length of his bare body, stopping just short of immodesty.

"Hello." She was softness itself, her voice rising from her bruised throat in a husky whisper.

Shiloh closed his eyes, running his hand through his shaggy hair, pushing it from his forehead. When he opened them again she was still there; he hadn't dreamed her.

She sat by his bed, dressed in a long painter's shirt and jeans. A black sketch pad and pens lay by her side. Her hands were folded demurely in her lap. The murky water of the quarry had been washed from her hair. It gleamed like stars on the canopy of the darkest night. With a scarf at her throat hiding the ravages of yesterday she was the image of tranquillity.

"You shouldn't be here." He found his voice. "You should be in bed."

"Jeb said you were sleeping. I wanted to be here when you woke."

"He should've stopped you."

"Nothing could've stopped me. Not even a dunderheaded fool."

"Dunderhead..." His chest heaved in an inaudible groan. "Last night. You heard." He closed his eyes again and waited.

"Enough."

"Meg, I..." What could he say to her? What was left was hers to say. Dread turned in him like a corkscrew. He didn't want to hear, but he must. He owed her that. Her cup of heart's blood. Betrayal's reckoning.

She was so close. Light shimmered around her. Her fragrance surrounded him. He wanted to touch her. He couldn't.

It hurt. It was what he deserved.

Hurt. Like the fool she called him he hadn't understood about loving and hurting. Only when she'd lain dazed and half frozen had the dam burst. Then, too late, he'd nearly suffocated in the torrent of what he needed to tell her, all he wanted her to know.

Had she come to mock his humble words, to throw them back at him and laugh in his face? "Meg." A rasping breath sawed at his throat. "Why are you here?"

She didn't answer. An odd smile curved her lips as her eyes roved over him. The unruly havoc he knew his fingers had created in his hair seemed a source of quiet amusement. Her smile changed, softened, when she studied his face, his craggy features, the damnable scar that marred them. He felt her blue-green gaze lingering an eternity at his mouth.

Chafing under that silent perusal, Shiloh shifted. He lifted himself into a sitting position with his back against the pillows. His motion turned her interest from his face.

Eyes that were deepening to green that had once meant passion slid in a slow look down his throat to his bare chest. Her smile faded. "You're hurt!" There was a catch in her voice, and something trembled in the broken tone. "No one told me."

"It's nothing. Scratches, a cut or two, a few bruises." He spoke more gruffly than he intended. "The doc said I'd live."

She recoiled at the last, and he could have kicked himself. Her memories of death and dying were too fresh for levity. There was sadness in her face and a sudden quietness as she continued to examine slowly and meticulously each battered inch of him. When he could bear no more of her strange mood he asked again, huskily, "What do you want, Meg? Why have you come?"

"I came to say thank you, and to celebrate my life with the man who gave it back to me."

Celebrate! An odd way to say she was glad to be alive. An odd word for gratitude. Shiloh felt agony billowing in him like a seething, black fog, blocking the light from his day. How hollow was gratitude when it was her love he needed. "I don't deserve your thanks," he said thickly. "I don't want your gratitude."

"Then what is it you want, Shiloh? Tell me. Forget guilt and impossible promises, forget everything but what's in your heart."

"It doesn't matter what I want."

"Yes, it does."

"No."

"Yes, dammit! It matters. It matters to you. It matters to me." She stood abruptly, stalking away, trembling in anger. Whirling around, she turned on him, her eyes blazing wildfire. "Why won't you say it?"

The deep-rooted sensations began. Tremors in the

pit of his stomach, an ache in his groin. He wanted Meg, and she knew it. But she intended to have the words.

His lashes dragged down, brushing his scarred and bruised cheeks, shielding his thoughts. "I want..." He shook his head, a lock of hair falling over his forehead. He couldn't say it, not to hear her laugh.

"You want me," Meg said, relenting when she saw his pain.

"No!"

"Yes."

There was a wonderful gentleness in her contradiction. Her footsteps approached, her hand brushed back the hair from his forehead. The bed dipped beneath her weight as she sat beside him.

"Shiloh, look at me."

Lashes fluttered and lifted. He found himself looking into a lovely face that held no mockery.

"Look at me," she repeated, shaking back her hair, her arms raised, unfettered breasts thrusting joyously against the soft cling of her shirt. "I'm alive. I'm well. Because of you."

"And Jeb and Jingo."

"Shh." Her hand stopped his lips, lingered to stray over his face. "This was for me," she murmured, her fingers like falling petals, touching the bruise on his cheek. "And this. And this."

Shiloh shivered as she explored, tracing the path of an angry welt, skirting a darkening bruise. She was driving him beyond his endurance. His skin flushed with the heat of arousal; his body clenched against it. "Meg, don't."

"Meg, don't." She laughed. Even as hoarse as she was, it was a musical sound. "How many times have I heard that? How many times have you worried about me, and look at what you've done to yourself. For me."

"If it hadn't been for my hateful arrogance, none of this would've happened." The veins in his neck were distended, and he was ashen and aching with the effort he made.

"Were you responsible for Ballenger's madness? Or Miss Hillyard's gossip? Or Mrs. Holcomb's misguided kindness?" Her hand trailed over the fold of the crumpled sheet, coming to rest low on his abdomen. Fuel for the fire that engulfed him.

"You're mortal, Shiloh. You're not God." Her injured voice had grown weaker, yet she continued. "You built an impregnable fortress around us. Ballenger could never have touched me if I hadn't broken my word and left the grounds."

"You did what you had to do. What any mother would. If...if things had been different, if I hadn't driven you away, you would've turned to me."

"You're wrong. Panic made me act as I did, not the strain between us. My children were gone. My mind was an empty wasteland. You didn't exist for me."

Shiloh flinched. A low, strangled sound was not hidden by the arm he dragged over his face.

"No!" Her hand glided up his body to cup his

cheek before moving from him. "It wasn't just you. It was myself, the world, everything. Nothing existed but his flowers, the note and my children. All I understood was that I had to follow instructions or lose them."

"They were safe all along. Delayed at the library by Alexis's slashed tire so you would believe his hoax."

She made no excuses, ducking her head in admission of the truth. "I was the unthinking fool, but," she said so quietly he hardly heard, "when I needed you, you came."

"You thought I wouldn't." God! Would he ever forget the sad, weak voice, the pale, beautiful face, the deadly water?

"No. Deep down, beyond fear and shattered pride, I knew you would be there."

"You believed?" *Believed in me!* A sudden wind twisted through the tree by his window, setting the leaves into a crisp rattle, taking up the chant spinning like trapped sunlight in his mind. *In me. In me.*

"As surely as I now believe I was never responsible for the consequences of Keith's drinking."

Shiloh sucked in a startled breath but said nothing. Incredibly Meg was calmly saying goodbye to guilt. To Keith.

"You spoke of a time bomb ticking. I thought you were wrong. Now I see. Hindsight is perfect, isn't it?" There was a shading of self-mockery in the garbled cliché. It was gone when she continued, "Keith's life was a series of prisons. The orphanages, the foster homes. Vietnam was the worst. It stunted his sense of self-worth. He'd been locked away from the real world for too long.

"Before me he never had anyone, not to call his own. He'd never learned to share. There was never the chance."

Her words were a breathy singsong, her sentences choppy, conserving the effort it took to force them through her tight throat. Only her quiet urgency kept him from begging her to stop.

"The fuse was armed. I became his obsession. He loved the children, but he hated them, too, because he thought they took a part of me from him. A third child was too much. He dealt with it by drinking. Nothing I could've said would change him."

"Nothing." Shiloh ventured a solemn assurance that went unnoticed.

"When I told him I had to leave, I'd done all I could. It was my only choice. I didn't kill the Ballengers or Keith." Slipping the ring from her finger she laid it on the bedside table. "I don't need any reminders."

She stopped as if she were finished, a chapter of her life completed. But Shiloh knew there was more. He waited.

"Our years together weren't what I imagined they were, but there were happy times. Keith wasn't a bad man. He was a good man who lost his way. The best of him still lives in his children."

Shiloh heard the peace of letting go. The ending of

one life so another could begin. "There would've been a day when he was proud they were his."

"Would he be proud to be their father now?"

"I think he would."

"Would you?"

"If they were mine, I'd be the proudest man on earth, and the happiest."

"Even if they're not of your blood?"

"It wouldn't matter." Eyes as blue as a summer morning's sky met hers. There was love in them. "It doesn't matter."

"Alexis is with them," she said as she stood, her hands going to the band of her jeans. "She swore on her life she'd see that young Miss Columbus wouldn't go exploring. We'll have to watch her closely, you know. She has a wonderful sense of adventure that mustn't be lost. Curbed, but not destroyed. Can you imagine what it will be like when she's sixteen and we..."

Shiloh wasn't listening to her monologue. His attention was on her clever, busy fingers, on the shapely legs visible as she slid her jeans down her hips and stepped out of them. Roughly he muttered, "Meg! What are you doing?"

"Isn't it obvious?" She looked up from a button on her shirt. "I'm undressing."

"Oh." Shiloh felt as if the breath had been knocked from him.

Meg returned to the buttons. "Jeb promised to help, and Jingo. You heard his helicopter, didn't you? Cass is putting Dakota out to pasture. Caroline and

Gabe are back. By the way, I met him, he's a terrific man, perfect for Caroline. Anyway, they have Shiloh Mark and our Portuguese friend out by the pool. If all else fails, the Jingo bird should keep our wandering miss put.''

''Does...'' Shiloh swallowed, his throat jerking convulsively. He was, indeed, wondering where his next breath was coming from. ''Does everyone know you're here?''

''Yes, even Mrs. Holcomb.'' Only one button was left. ''Any more questions?''

''Just one.'' He sat very still, his hungry eyes on her.

''Ask.''

''Do you have anything on under that shirt?''

''Not a thing.'' Slowly she slid it from her shoulders, letting it fall with the scarf to join her jeans.

Shiloh had tossed back the sheet intending to stand, but confronted by the vision that had haunted his days as well as his nights, he sank down on the edge of the bed. The faded darkness of the barn hadn't betrayed him. She was as lovely as he'd dreamed. There was no more enchanting woman.

Now, as in the shadowy half light of the barn, he discovered how much she pleased him. How perfect her body was for his. How she could stir a need that was as tender as it was savage.

She was his! She knew it. She must!

She had to know her full, perfect breasts were meant for his worshiping hand, the tawny crest his to suckle. Her slender midriff, flowing like sweet music to the curve of waist and taut belly, invited his caress. The secret shadow at the juncture of her thighs promised heaven only to him.

"You're beautiful. Too beautiful." Doubting the strength of his legs, he wound his hands in her hair, drawing her down to his lap. He pressed her head to his chest, her cheek against his pounding heart.

"If your intention is to drive me mad, you've done it. Do you feel what you do to me?" he rasped. "Do you hear? I didn't think there was anyone in the world like you. Not for me."

She laughed softly, not intimidated by his harsh manner. "I warned you before this ended you would think I was a witch." Rubbing her cheek against the downy pelt that covered his chest, nipping at a tiny nipple, she was rewarded by a ragged gasp.

Trembling, Shiloh stroked the length of her back, his palms sculpting the curve of her buttocks and down her thigh as it lay over his. The heat from her body rose to him, filling him with the scent of her. "Witch, witch," he groaned, cradling her in his arms, holding her closer. "I thought I'd lost you. The note, those damnable flowers, the quarry. The water, cold, dark. Oh, God! I couldn't find you."

"You did," Meg soothed, her lips brushing his burning flesh. "I knew you would."

Shiloh's hand was in her hair, stroking it, tangling it, holding her willingly captive. "I love you," he whispered against the pulse at her temple. "Now I know I have for three long years."

Meg was quiet, too quiet. It frightened him. Had

he said too much? With his hands at her shoulders he set her from him. His frown deepened at the tears that spangled her wonderful eyes. With a palm he stroked her wet cheek. "Why, sweetheart?"

A tear that clung to her lashes spilled down her cheek over his fingers. "Because you're so beautiful."

Shiloh's startled laugh was cut short. Suddenly he understood. Meg looked at his ravaged face as if it were perfect, because she saw him through the eyes of love.

"God! I want you. I want to make love to you, but Ballenger..." He shook his head. "I don't want to hurt you."

"I'll heal, I've begun already, and that word has been used too much between us," she said softly. "There are all kinds of hurts. Good ones. Bad ones. Wonderful ones." She took his hand in hers, placing it low on her abdomen. "I have a hurt here, and only you can ease it."

"Me?" he whispered, his fingers stroking the gently rounded curve of her belly. "Stupid, dunderheaded Shiloh Butler?"

"You." She gasped and arched against him as he explored further. "Wonderful, handsome, *slow* Shiloh Butler."

"Slow?" He smiled in his wanderings. "As in inert?"

"Hardly." She moved languorously in his lap and savored the groan he could not stifle. "As in you're driving me crazy."

''We can't have that now, can we?'' His hand was at her breast, his thumb teasing a nipple to the full bloom of a rose.

''Shiloh!''

He laughed and tumbled with her into the sheets. His laughter was the second most beautiful thing in the world, Meg thought dreamily. When his laughter stopped and his body joined with hers was the first.

Meg woke. The sun had moved beyond the window. They had slept for hours. She stretched. Her body was one delicious ache. Her outstretched hands touched Shiloh's empty pillow. Brushing her hair from her face, she leaned on one arm. He stood by the window, his back to her. He hadn't dressed. Beaten and battered, honed to a fine edge by their troubles, he was still the most marvelous man.

''Hey,'' she called quietly. ''What are you doing way over there?''

''I was thinking about Jeb.''

''He was magnificent yesterday.''

''He was saving my lady.''

''Is that what you call me?''

''Do I have the right?''

''You have every right, I wouldn't be here if you didn't.''

He turned to her. ''Does that mean...''

''It means whatever you want it to mean.''

His heart soared. He had never been so incredibly happy. ''Oh, God! Sweetheart.'' He went to her, his hands burrowing in the midnight fall of hair he loved so much. "Don't ever leave me. Be my wife. Give me your children. Let me love them. Let me love you. I won't ask for anything else. Just stay with me."

"I'll stay," she promised.

"For as long as I want you?"

"For as long," Meg whispered. She had much to tell him. Much to teach him. About himself. About loving. But that could come later. Much, much later. "I love you, Shiloh," she murmured as she drew him down to her. "That's the celebration of my life."

"Forever?" His lips caressed hers.

"Forever," Meg murmured, waiting for him as a flower waits for the sun.

"And longer," Shiloh promised, and began with her the journey to the enchanted place that only wounded angels know.

* * * * *

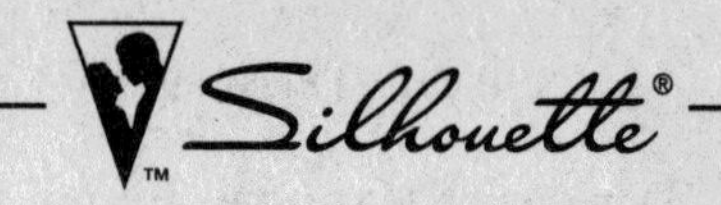

Silhouette®
SPECIAL EDITION™

Emotional, compelling stories that capture the intensity of living, loving and creating a family in today's world.

Modern, passionate reads that are powerful and provocative.

Dramatic and sensual tales of paranormal romance.

Romances that are sparked by danger and fueled by passion.

Visit Silhouette Books at www.eHarlequin.com

SDIR07